MURDER ON SAINT CHARLES AVENUE

BY ROBERT TAYLOR

Murder on Saint Charles Avenue, © 2019
By Robert Taylor
ISBN: 978-0-578-60901-0

Edited by, Maisah Robinson and Christine LePorte
Cover Art by, Eric Nava

ACKNOWLEDGMENTS

Thanks to Maria, my wife, for her patience, love, and steady encouragement to complete this project. Thanks also to my good friend Paul Janoff, for providing sound advice and thoughtful suggestions as the book reached fruition. Based solely on my mental sense of what the front and back book cover design should look like, thanks to Eric Nava for his skill as an illustrator to bring it to reality.

DEDICATION

This novel is dedicated to all fellow first-time authors who possess the desire and ability to express themselves vividly in writing while providing entertainment for the reader. Writing can be enjoyable while stretching one's imagination. Vivid thoughts and ideas can be captured on a blank sheet of paper for the creation and enjoyment of others.

ROBERT TAYLOR

FOREWORD

This story unfolds because of an intense desire to personally express creativity and suspense while providing the reader with the enjoyment of surprise and maybe even a degree of shock. As a young man, I never considered creativity to be my forte. During my professional life, after military retirement, I realized that I had underestimated my creative abilities. Through a series of experiences and work assignments, I unexpectedly exhibited clear indications of genuine sparks of exceptional creativity. To coin a phrase: "Where there's a spark, there must be a degree of talent."

As a result, those sparks of creativity served as an encouragement to explore and write about some of my unique thoughts and ideas. I was determined to demonstrate these sparks of creativity and suspense as expressed in words. Those very sparks were the epiphany that inspired and encouraged me to write and publish my memoir, titled **Times and Events in the Life of Robert Taylor**. This novel that you are about to read captures suspense, intrigue, surprise, and maybe even a degree of shock, but you, the reader, will be the best judge of that.

CONTENTS

PROLOGUE

Alan Jared is a successful writer who has authored and published several bestselling mystery novels. Alan met Jason Beale by coincidence on a private beach while vacationing on the island of St. Barts. They both sunbathed daily and enjoyed the warmth of the sand against their backs. As a result of their sudden friendship, they met for private dinners on the beach each evening, helping to solidify their mutual attraction.

Jason found himself smitten by Alan's tall and slender physique, along with the olive skin associated with his Mediterranean ancestry. Even more alluring to Jason were Alan's femininity and keen facial features. Beyond the physical, Jason was enamored by Alan's intellect, personality, and charm. He was especially attracted to Alan because of his business prowess and success as a published author several times over, which was accompanied by obvious personal wealth. Not that Jason needed money—far from it—rather, he was glad to be with someone who wasn't looking for a sugar daddy.

Alan and Jason struck up such a close friendship that they consummated their relationship in fairly short order. Jason learned more of Alan's wealth, as represented by his posh homes located in San Francisco and Palm Springs. Alan spoke often about his sixty-foot yacht and other material assets. He invited Jason to set sail with him on the yacht in the future. They parted ways after the vacation, but swore to stay in touch via social media. Overtime, their emotions took a stronger grip on their relationship.

As they chatted one day via visual social media, Jason poured his heart out, "Absence makes the heart grow fonder, and that is exactly what's occurring with me, as I daydream about us."

Alan quickly agreed, "Yes, I must admit that I feel the same way about you, but absence can also make the heart wander. We must remain in the moment and consolidate our lives within the same general geographic location."

As their emotional bond became stronger, it became clear that they must live closer to one another. This would be complicated, however, because Alan could continue to write from almost anywhere in the world, but Jason was held to a desk in New Orleans because of his co-ownership of FA&O Shipping LLC.

Alan reached a decision--to best continue their love affair, he would relocate from San Francisco to New Orleans. As a result, Alan planned to purchase a new home in New Orleans, while retaining the mansion he owned in the exclusive area of San Francisco known as Seacliff. Once Alan arrived in the Big Easy, it wasn't long before he closed on the sale of a beautiful Victorian mansion originally built in 1872. It was a stellar choice, because the mansion had many of the original details, including a wrap-around porch, and an exquisite *porte cochere* that carriages use to pass under. Alan was bustling with excitement as he shopped antique stores for furnishings, and found ornate treasures, such as a Queen Anne secretary desk, antique Peking wool rugs, and Victorian carved walnut armchairs. To keep the mansion running smoothly, Alan hired a fulltime gardener and house keeper.

Jason was a frequent visitor to Alan's new home, sometimes spending the night after enjoying an intimate dinner on the outdoor patio of the residence. Alan had made a sizeable investment in emotion and capital to be a fixture in Jason's life. They were committed to one another in love and often spoke of the advantages and disadvantages of marriage. However, Alan was unaware of Jason's entangled, past love life.

CHAPTER ONE

Jeff Gaskins is a gigolo of sorts, standing well over six feet tall and weighing at least 225 pounds, crowned by a thick head of long blond hair that he grooms Kennedy style. He spends most of his days exercising in the gym as a weightlifter and bodybuilder. He takes great pride in his physique. Several years ago, Jason Beale committed to marry Jeff and to provide him with all the necessities of life, without the requirement to work. He also gave Jeff a generous monthly spending account and credit cards. While he hadn't yet married Jeff, to show further commitment to him, Jason also opened investment accounts to ensure that Jeff wouldn't want for anything, ever.

It's a beautiful evening as Alan entertains Jason in his beautiful Victorian mansion. When Jason's cell phone rings, he immediately recognizes the number. He always knew Jeff would one day call at the most inopportune time, while he and Alan were together. Jason dreads answering Jeff's call, but he responds with: "Hello."

Jeff says, "It's me, how have you been?"

Alan stares at Jason as he nervously speaks into the telephone: "Please hold a moment." He covers the phone with his hand and excuses himself from Alan's presence, telling him, "It's an urgent business call."

Jason steps into an adjoining room as he begins speaking to Jeff. He whispers, "This is not a convenient time to talk."

Jeff says, "I need to see you tonight, so what time will you be available? And why are you whispering?"

Jason replies, "Not tonight, Jeff, I'm busy."

Sensing something is awry, Jeff becomes angry and asserts, "I'm coming over right now! What the fuck is going on, Jason?"

"No, you cannot come over right now," Jason hisses. "I will speak with you sometime tomorrow." He ends the call and places the ringer on vibrate to silence any other disturbing calls from Jeff. Jason returns to where Alan is relaxing and apologizes for his brief absence.

Alan says with a nervous smile, "If I didn't know any better, I'd think you were talking to a lover." Jason returns the smile but says nothing.

Jason isn't sure how best to proceed with breaking things off with Jeff. To take such action would entail closing his credit cards and investment accounts. Sudden loss of Jeff's total dependency on Jason for his livelihood would be a very unpleasant situation for both of them. Without a doubt, Jeff will be disappointed, not to mention furious, especially after an enjoyable three-year monogamous relationship. He would have to find a job and finance his own living expenses.

The thought of this sudden assault on Jeff's livelihood makes Jason quiver. He can't get the courage to meet with Jeff to break the bad news about their breakup.

He is terrified of telling Jeff that they're finished and all of his financial support will be gone, forever. In an effort to avoid a confrontation, Jason writes a letter explaining his reasons for breaking up and the resulting consequences of that action.

Jason mails the letter to the home of Jeff's parents, where Jeff has lived all of his life. Two days later, Jeff receives and opens Jason's letter.

Dear Jeff,

It is with great sadness and trepidation that I inform you of my decision to end our relationship after 3 years of sharing time, space, and wonderful events with you. The specific reason for parting ways with you is because someone else occupies that special emotional place in my heart that you controlled during our years together. As a result, I can no longer be involved with you in any manner. Because my affections warmly reside with someone else, I'm obligated to foreclose our relationship. Because of my decision and a new path forward, I have taken the necessary action to close certain joint investment accounts. Please also know that all debt associated with credit cards in your possession has been retired and the accounts have been closed. It is painful to say this, but

please do not attempt to contact me in any way, shape, or form. I wish you well.
Sincerely, Jason

As Jason expected, Jeff is incensed by the contents of the letter. It doesn't require a feat of mental gymnastics for him to realize that he is destitute and without money for the necessities of life. He pounds his fist on the sturdy mahogany dining table in his parents' kitchen. He is especially livid at Jason's uncaring tone in the letter. His face is crimson and displays an angry scowl, beads of sweat covered his brow.

The next morning, Jeff picks up his cell phone and dials a number. The phone rings on the other end and is quickly answered by Jason, "Good morning, Jeff, but we don't have anything to discuss."

"You can't do this to me, Jason. After what we meant to each other you send such a cold and heartless letter? I have no money for food, clothing, gym membership, or even gas for my car. You know full well that I've depended on you for my livelihood for years."

Jason is emotionally drained as he tries to calmly explain, "Jeff, all good things must eventually come to an end. We had a wonderful and productive life together, many times over. Throughout that time, I demonstrated my generosity to address your basic needs. I am under no obligation to continue providing such largesse."

Jeff heaves a sigh that Jason can hear through the phone. "Fine. But can you at least find it in your heart to lend me some money until I get a job and can pay you back?"

Jason is firm, responding with, "No." Then he adds, "By the way, Jeff, I requested in my letter that you not contact me under any circumstances, so please honor that request."

Jeff angrily retorts, "So you think that after a three-year relationship, you can just flick me off with a finger as if I'm an insect on your sleeve? Well, you can't, Jason, and you'll regret treating me like this!" Jeff's voice rises as he shouts his final message into the phone: "Fuck you!" Then the phone goes dead silent. But does this silence their relationship?

In the ensuing days, weeks, and months, Jason is relieved that Jeff has honored his request that he not contact him again. Because Jason no longer feels frightened by Jeff's threat as communicated during their last telephone conversation, he has entered into a life of harmony and happiness with Alan. Jeff is unskilled, but has managed to find a minimum wage job at a local car wash, detailing high end vehicles. Although Jeff has found a job and accepted his life circumstance, has he forgiven Jason for the meanspirited and uncaring manner in which their relationship ended? Maybe not.

***

Jason and Jeff live in New Orleans, known as "The Big Easy," which is comprised of a broad cross-section of ethnicities, religions, tastes, and lifestyles. The city is home to some 391,000 people and the best place to savor a cup of chicory coffee, and world`-famous beignets at Cafe Du Monde French Market. On the morning of February 11th, the air is a bit chilly. A well-dressed man wearing a gray fedora, matching leather gloves, and a long black overcoat walks along Saint Charles Avenue. He's concerned about his business meeting scheduled for this morning. Because he's in no hurry to arrive at his destination, he walks at a moderate pace, his outer clothing providing warmth and comfort sufficient to ward off the cold. The man is focused on a timely arrival at his predetermined destination, a mansion located at 4701 Saint Charles Avenue. He understands the importance of punctuality in business, so he plans to arrive a few minutes early. He anticipates that his business with the mansion's resident will conclude in just a few minutes, resulting in personal wealth, satisfaction, and colossal business success.

As the man arrives at his destination, he looks up at the imposing front façade of the mansion. The siding on the building is painted a bright beige. The mansion and grounds, featuring a beautiful black wrought iron fence bordering the veranda, appear warm and inviting. Using both of his gloved hands, the man pushes through the otherwise cold wrought iron gate leading to the front yard of the premises.

After striding along the flagstone walkway, he arrives at a staircase constructed of stone. He ascends several steps and then walks across the veranda to arrive at the front door. Without hesitating or ringing the doorbell, the man punches a five-digit code into the security panel for the home alarm system, located to the left of the entryway. An audible click sounds and the door silently swings open to the inside without human intervention. The man walks in beyond the threshold and immediately views the interior of the open space. As he steps further into the mansion, he is awestruck by the eclectic works of art consisting of one of Andy Warhol's Mao Zedong portraits, a Picasso, and an Amedeo Modigliani painting.

The large open space is populated by tastefully placed collectibles, some from Barneys of New York. Just one of the exquisite vases could be fenced for over five thousand dollars. But the man has other important business on his mind at the moment, business that must be completed this day. The house is eerily quiet, and he navigates carefully and quietly, not to create a disturbance. He closes the door behind him and advances down a long corridor to his right, at the end of which he arrives at a sitting room. As he gazes into the room, the visitor sees a man who appears to be sleeping on an eighteenth-century Camelback sofa. The man's stertorous breathing suggests that he is in a state of deep sleep. As expected at this hour of the day, the apparent owner of the mansion is napping and has left himself physically vulnerable. Not wanting to disturb or awaken the sleeper, the man quietly takes several measured steps in the direction of the sofa.

The visitor is but one step away, when suddenly he withdraws from under his overcoat a long double-bladed knife. Silently, and without hesitation, the man plunges the blade into the chest of the sleeping man, aiming for his heart. Bursting with a murderous energy, he once more thrusts his blade with great force into the chest of his victim, as blood spurts from the deeply penetrating wounds. The exterior of the man's coat is subsequently splattered with blood. The man stands there as if admiring his dastardly work, but he's looking for signs of life. Once certain the sleeper will not recover from the assault, he removes his gloves and long coat. To conceal the splotches of blood, he turns his coat outside in and places his gloves

11

and the long blade of death within. After a final visual assessment of the area and his victim to ensure death is absolute and that no trace evidence is left behind, he neatly folds his coat across his outstretched arm. The man calmly retraces his original footsteps toward the front door without touching anything or attempting to gather valuable collectibles. On his way out, he remembers to wipe the inner and outer door handles clean of latent fingerprints. The man quietly escapes into the city, the din punctuated by the loud creaking generated by the steel wheels of streetcars rolling along Saint Charles Avenue.

CHAPTER TWO

The stately mansion at 4701 Saint Charles Avenue is adjoined by a two-story structure, which occupies 2,500 square feet of space in the rear. The first floor of the spacious structure is reserved to accommodate six luxury vehicles. The second floor serves as living quarters for Mr. and Mrs. Dima Ivanov. Mr. Ivanov has been the longtime gardener, handyman, and chauffeur, while his wife is responsible for housekeeping, cooking, running errands, and performing other tasks, as necessary. The second-floor living space is fully equipped with a full range of appliances that are provided without charge. The couple are long-term residents and employees of the mansion. They have been motivated and committed to working at their jobs for many years due to the generous monthly financial compensation in exchange for services rendered.

They are pleased with their employment and living arrangements.

The workday for the couple started late this morning because the owner of the mansion, Mr. Beale, made it clear the previous evening that he would be involved in a very important business meeting with a client. As a result, he had been adamant that he didn't want to be disturbed in any way until late afternoon. Mr. Beale lives alone and enjoys a solitary lifestyle. Visiting guests at the mansion are only a few who receive an invitation, the uninvited are turned away.

This morning, Mrs. Ivanov is first to reach the mansion after walking the flagstone path leading from the living quarters located in the rear of the mansion. Her husband closely follows. It is just before noon. Mrs. Ivanov intends to start preparing lunch for Mr. Beale and a possible guest.

Reaching the rear entrance to the mansion, she taps the appropriate five-digit code into the security panel near the rear door entrance. After an audible click, the door springs open automatically. She tiptoes into the mansion so as not to disturb Mr. Beale. She stops in the kitchen for a few seconds to listen but hears nothing, all silence. She wants to make Mr. Beale aware of her presence and let him know she is ready to work. If she hears voices or observes someone other than Mr. Beale, she will leave to give him more undisturbed time for him to complete his business. Hearing nothing, she walks down a long hallway and turns to her right where the sitting room is located.

Mr. Ivanov, who entered the mansion moments after his wife, suddenly hears a loud screeching noise like one emitted from some wild animal. He immediately recognizes the agonizing sound as coming from his wife.

As he hurries along the hallway to respond to his wife's chilling screams, he observes her moving quickly away from the sitting room. Her face is aghast in terror, as she presses her hands tightly over her mouth to suppress her screams.

Puzzled, Mr. Ivanov immediately flings his arms around his distraught wife to comfort her. He then firmly grabs her by the arms and nervously asks in his Russian accent: "What's the matter, honey?"

With a trembling hand, Mrs. Ivanov points in the direction of the sitting room and shakes her head from side to side. Frowning, Mr. Ivanov moves past his wife to look into the sitting room. He gazes upon seeing the gruesome image of Mr. Beale, and is horrified to see him covered in blood. The Camelback sofa is also splattered with blood, some of which trails onto the carpet, forming a small puddle.

Mr. Ivanov hurries back to the kitchen, where his wife is now sitting at a dining table, shocked and grief-stricken., Mr. Ivanov quickly calls 911. In response to the police dispatcher's voice, he frantically explains, "There has been a horrible accident here at my place of work. Please send the police and an ambulance. Mr. Jason Beale is dead, I believe." He shakily returns the receiver on the hook and turns to console his wife, without hearing the probing questions from the dispatcher on the other end of the line.

As the death of his employer weighs heavily on his mind and heart, Dima Ivanov recalls how good Jason Beale treated him and his wife. He was kind, thoughtful, and very generous. How could anyone in their right mind act in such a vile and vicious manner, resulting in the death of Mr. Beale?

***

Over the next few weeks, Mr. Beale's death will be investigated by the highly specialized group of detectives at the Criminal Investigations Division (CID) of the New Orleans Police Department. The chief homicide detective for the Criminal Investigation Division of the New Orleans Police Department is Arthur Beauregard, who has been a cop for twenty-five years, while working the homicide detail for eighteen of those years. He is affectionately and simply known amongst friends and peers as Art. He is quickly donning his coat when his partner, Jack Fratelli, a fifteen-year veteran of the department, enters the busy squad room. Jack immediately hears Art's loud and commanding voice: "We just got a call for a possible crime on Saint Charles Avenue. Let's go!"

As Art and Jack arrive at the Mansion, the customary police cruisers and coroner's vehicle are already on the scene. Yellow crime scene tape cordons off the boundary of the mansion, keeping out the gawkers and onlookers who are milling around on the street out front.

An older couple is nervously waiting in the kitchen as the crime scene investigation gets underway. Art and Jack approach the couple, Mr. and Mrs. Ivanov, according to another officer. After introducing himself and Jack, Art asks, "What happened here?"

Mrs. Ivanov, with a distant look on her face, shrugs her shoulders. "I don't know."

Mr. Ivanov is more forthcoming, "We don't know what happened. We entered the mansion and almost right away found Mr. Beale covered in blood on the couch. I called the police."

Art asks the couple if they saw anything unusual or heard any strange noises. Both shake their heads while responding with a barely audible "No."

"Does anyone else live in the mansion?" asks Art.

"No, Mr. Beale lived alone. He wasn't married."

"What about his next of kin?" asks Jack.

At this point, Mrs. Ivanov interjects, "Mr. Beale was scheduled to have a meeting with someone earlier this morning, but he didn't say with whom."

Speaking clearly and listening attentively, Jack probes, "Was it a normal practice for Mr. Beale to conduct business here in the mansion?"

Again, the couple responds in unison with a shake of the head and "No."

"How long have you worked for Mr. Beale?"

"Both Mrs. Ivanov and I have lived and worked here since the mansion was renovated by Mr. Beale...that must have been our first year here, back in 2001."

"Does he have any known enemies or anyone who would want to hurt him?".

"No one that we know of.".

"Did you notice any money, jewelry, or other valuables missing from the residence?"

"We haven't looked, Detective.".

"Can you tell us anything about Mr. Beale's friends who might have visited the mansion?"

Mrs. Ivanov immediately blurted out "There was a younger man who I saw once or twice, I think." He visited mainly in the evening."

"Do you know the man's name?"

"I'm not sure, but I think I may have heard the name Alan."

Jack pushes, "Do you remember Alan's last name?"

"I'm not sure, Detective."

"Could you identify Alan if you saw him in person or a picture?

"Maybe, but I'm not sure. He was tall, a little under six feet maybe, with sort of light, tan skin, I think they call it a café-au-lait complexion."

"Was there much of a party life or any entertainment events conducted at the mansion?"

Again, and in unison, the couple quietly and somberly respond with the word "No," while simultaneously shaking their heads.

"Would you please explain the circumstances under which you discovered Mr. Beale's body?"

Mr. Ivanov gave an account of the workday, "The day started later than normal for us because last night, Mr. Beale said that early this morning he would be involved in a very important business meeting. "Mr. Beale made it very clear that he was expecting a client to discuss a sensitive legal matter, and didn't want to be disturbed in any way until later in the afternoon."

"Was Mr. Beale an attorney? And if so, where did he work?"

"I believe he was chief counsel and co-owner of the company. It's a big company. I believe it was called FA&O shipping."

"Thanks for answering our questions. You can go now." Art and Jack offer their business cards, and Jack tells them to "Please don't hesitate to contact us if you have anything else that might help us solve this case."

"We will, sir" both of them reply.

A patrolman gestures to Art that he wants to speak with him. The patrolman and Art step aside, and the patrolman reports, "We canvassed the neighborhood, asking the standard questions. We came up negative, except for an elderly lady who claims to have seen a man wearing a gray fedora and black coat walking along Saint Charles Avenue. She thought he seemed out of place. Other neighbors confirmed that she's a kind of a busybody, watching everything in the immediate neighborhood from her first-floor front window."

"What's her name and address?"

"Pauline Clifton, 4712 Saint Charles Avenue."

"Did she say anything else?"

"She described a tall man wearing a hat and dark coat. That's all I have, Lieutenant."

"Okay, thanks," says Art.

Just as Pauline Clifton was preparing a light snack, her doorbell rings, then she cautiously answers the door. Art and Jack are standing there, stern-faced, with just a hint of a smile.

"How may I help you, gentlemen?" she asks. To Art and Jack, Pauline appears to be in her early to mid-sixties, with a face lined with experience and wisdom.

"Good afternoon, Ms. Clifton. I'm Lieutenant Detective Arthur Beauregard and this is my partner, Sergeant Detective Jack Fratelli. We're with the New Orleans Police Department."

As they flash their badges, she invites them to "Please come in and have a seat."

As they cross the threshold into the home, they can't help but notice that it is tastefully decorated with expensive late colonial, and Pennsylvania Dutch antique furnishings, complemented by valuable artwork by such world-renowned artists giants, such as Paul Gauguin and Jackson Pollock. Once they're seated, Ms. Clifton offers the detectives herb tea or chicory coffee, which they politely decline.

Art gets to the point, "Ms. Clifton, ma'am, as you might have guessed, we're here about the incident that occurred earlier today across the street."

"Oh yes, my heavens," Ms. Clifton responds.

"We understand that you spoke with one of our police officers and gave him a statement, is that correct?" Art asks.

"Yes, I did, young man."

"Can you tell us what you saw?"

"Well, as I told the officer, I saw a tall man wearing a gray hat and long dark coat."

Jack then wants to know, "why do you think he was in the neighborhood?"

"I don't know, he looked sort of creepy and a bit mysterious. He just wasn't the type of person from this area, if you know what I mean. I tend to see everything from my front window. As you can see from here, I can see almost to the end of the block from one end to the other. By the way, the man I saw had a tan complexion."

"Do you know what race his was--white, African American, Hispanic?" asks Art.

"I'm not so sure of that."

"And what time of day was it when you saw the man, Ms. Clifton?" Jack inquires.

"It was somewhere between ten thirty and about eleven o'clock this morning."

"Are you quite sure about the time, Ms. Clifton?"

As she turns her head and looks at Jack from the corner of her eye, she says, "I have a good feel for the time."

"Just one more thing, Ms. Clifton. Did you see anyone enter or leave the mansion today?"

"No, actually I didn't. Sometimes I'll have some tea or light snack brought in by the maid. That's the only time that I might have been distracted from the activity on the block."

As the detectives leave, Art thanks her for answering their questions, gave her their business cards and implore her to, "Please let us know if you should remember anything else that might help us with our investigation."

"Okay, I will." Pauline wondered whether there was a killer loose in the area. Not even a cup of chamomile tea would calm her nerves tonight.

Once in the squad car, Art declared, "We've got to find this guy, this Alan. He fits the physical profile provided by Mrs. Ivanov as well as Ms. Clifton."

"Yeah," Jack exclaimed. "He could be our perp!"

CHAPTER THREE

George Roberts, the chief of police, is outraged when he is informed of Jason Beale's death. Jason is one of the city's greatest benefactors, and happens to be on the mayor's list of very generous donors to his reelection campaign. The Chief knows that Mayor Austin will pressure him incessantly to solve this case and have someone convicted. Mayor Austin personally knows Mr. Beale, the wealthy co-owner of FA&O Shipping LLC, as he is a prominent figure in the local community and is well respected among high-profile attorneys and powerful, influential politicians. To combat any eventual criticism about the ineffectiveness of the New Orleans Police Department, the Chief decides to conduct a rare, televised news conference to inform the community of the tragic death of one of its most well-known and admired citizens.

From the Chief's perspective, conducting a televised news conference will also help to ensure the widest dissemination of his oratory skills and ability to get cases solved and criminals prosecuted. During the news conference, he will promise to levy all human capital and investigative resources necessary to solve this brutal and heinous crime.

Because the chief has joined the campaign for the position of mayor, he thinks of a news conference as tantamount to a free campaign outreach effort, and fortuitously will be funded by the department. His strategy for election is l convey the message and image of a man tough on crime, who teams up with progressive prosecutors known for winning cases. If elected Mayor, he promises to keep the citizens safe in their homes and the streets and ensure that the police force serve as guardians, rather than warriors. The crime statistics for New Orleans are staggering, the crime rate is 95% higher than the national average; daily, there are 14.7 crimes per 100,000 people. Because his focus is on crime-prevention, he just might garner a mass number of supporters from all walks of life for his campaign. There is much at stake and he must make certain he's scaling-up his campaign strategies to conquer his opponents.

It is on a somber, overcast day when the news conference begins, Captain Madelyn Grayson, Lieutenant Arthur Beauregard, and Detective Sergeant Jack Fratelli flank the Chief, who clears his throat and begins , "Today, I'm announcing the death of one of New Orleans's most prominent citizens: Mr. Jason Beale, who lived at 4701 Saint Charles Avenue, in the Garden District. Mr. Beale was kind, well liked, and respected within the community. He was also a generous donor to several worthy causes, which included food for the poor, the indigent, and homeless citizens of our city. He was a business owner, an attorney, and an employer of hundreds of people from diverse backgrounds. As Police Chief, I have taken action to ensure that all necessary resources are committed to apprehending, as quickly as possible, the killer or killers responsible for causing the untimely death of Mr. Beale. Are there any questions at this point?"

A reporter from NACK News piped up, "Chief Roberts, what was the manner of death?"

"We believe this is a homicide; however, the medical examiner will confirm the cause and manner of death."

"But Chief Roberts, could the cause of death be natural or accidental?"

"No, I don't think so, but again, this is subject to the medical examiner's findings."

"Chief, I'm Carol Baker with News12. Was the residence burglarized?"

"Not that we can tell at this point. We're still investigating all possible motives."

"Chief Roberts, Steve Bush with CNM TV News. Have you developed a suspect or suspects in the case?"

"No, not as yet, but we will."

"Chief, I'm Pete Bell from EPIC News. Was there a witness or possible witness to the crime that you can identify for us?"

"As part of our investigation, we're talking to neighbors in the area to help determine if they saw or heard anything unusual that could be related to the case. I'm confident that our investigation will eventually provide clues to the identity of possible suspects who may have been involved in the crime."

"Chief, I'm Ben Millard, with KEPT News. Does Mr. Beale have any family that you can tell us about?"

"I can tell you that Mr. Beale was a private man, and as best we can tell, he lived alone, and we have no record of next of kin. We're trying to secure that information."

When no further questions are forthcoming, the Chief closes out his news conference, "If anyone living in the area has seen or heard anything unusual near Mr. Beale's residence, please contact the Crime Tips Hotline at 200-821-2222. We appreciate any assistance from the community at large."

One of the prominent members of the community at large is Katherine Parchisi, an imposing figure, standing over six feet tall in her four-inch, Christian Louboutin stiletto heels with red-lacquered soles. She is a graduate of the University of San Francisco with a bachelor of science degree in human relations and organizational behavior. A successful law school admission test and subsequent acceptance of her application to attend Hastings College of the Law closely followed.

Katherine had many romantic relationships while studying law, but she resisted all efforts by both men and women to persuade and charm their way into her life. All such amorous efforts failed because Katherine was bent on preparing to join a prestigious law firm. Nonetheless, she was affable and willing to discuss the canons of law with anyone with the same career aspirations. She graduated summa cum laude, with a 4.25 grade point average, and was subsequently recruited to work at Taylor, Lorton, and Wharton Law Partners LLC, one of the most profitable, well-known law firms in the state, specializing in white collar defense, and intellectual property, securities and commercial liability litigation.

The two senior partners and vice president of the firm, Paul Nahm, Michael Blunt, and Judith Wilburn, respectively, conducted Katherine's initial job interview. They warmly greeted and introduced themselves to Katherine. As vice president of the firm, Judith welcomed her to the interview, "Good morning, Katherine, if we may refer to you by your first name?"

"Yes, please do so."

Judith continued in a controlled, professional manner, "We are acutely aware of your academic prowess while in law school, and graduating summa cum laude, which reflects your ability to succeed, despite any vicissitudes of life that you may encounter. You have all the qualifications necessary to join our firm. Now, we have but one complex, unique question. Please take a short period to carefully consider your response."

Without hesitation, Katherine answered, "Yes, I would be more than glad to."

After a brief, awkward pause, Judith confirmed, "Now that you are comfortable, we'll proceed. How would your worst enemy describe you, and if he or she were to ask you to defend them in a court of law for a capital crime, would you be willing to, and if so, why?"

Even though she was prepared for a unique question, Katherine was taken aback by the question, but remain composed and managed to give a coherent answer.

"Well, as you know, I'm sworn to the attorney's oath to support the Constitution of the United States, and that I will humble myself in the practice of law, as well as conducting myself with integrity and civility in dealing with and communicating with the court and all related parties. Moreover, since the client is willing to exchange my skill and expertise in the law for just financial compensation, it would require loyalty, allegiance, and deliverance of the best legal counsel and advice."

Katherine took a breath and then moved on with the next part of her answer. "As for the first half of your question, regarding what my worst enemy might say about me; if I were being fairly judged he or she might say something to the effect that I am very smart, fair-minded, sophisticated, legally competent, and sometimes impatient, curt, and demanding when important actions are not completed properly and in a timely manner. The latter would probably be the main reason an individual might harbor sufficient envy, animus, or dislike.

"At this point," Katherine continued, "I'm unaware of anyone that I would deem as an enemy, so my response is consistent with that thought and belief. This is my abbreviated response to your question, which I hope is sufficient, however, I'm prepared to expand upon my response, if necessary. As an obvious disclosure, I think it's reasonable to think that my ethnicity could potentially play a role in the creation of friends or enemies within the workplace, but please know and understand that I'm committed to establishing and maintaining a positive work situation and environment...no matter what it takes."

Judith quickly responded, "Katherine, if we had issues with your ethnicity, you might not be sitting in front of us at this very moment, and responding to our questions. The fact that you are African American has no bearing on your suitability to work for Taylor, Lorton, and Wharton LLC."

Judith went on, "Since you've captured our rapt attention, can you start work as early as next week?"

Katherine was surprised that the question had come so quickly and after such a short interview, but willingly accepted.

As soon as she began working at the firm, a few things became clear. Katherine Parchisi towered over most of the men and women there. She was statuesque and beautifully coiffed, her makeup always impeccably applied. Unbeknownst to Katherine, she was considered by certain men within the firm to be "stacked" and gifted with a feminine figure that was the envy of many female employees.

Having worked for the firm for a while now, she is considered untouchable by the men because she is already spoken for by Mr. Kenneth Blanchard. She is known to be professionally aggressive and exceedingly ambitious. After her work on several high-profile cases that she successfully litigated and won for clients and the firm, Katherine has become well respected and is soon understood to be the top litigator within the firm.

She is skilled in the art of persuasion through one of the greatest tools an attorney could ever possess: her "gift for gab." In record time, rumor has it that she will soon be considered for a coveted partnership within the firm.

CHAPTER FOUR

Forensic analysis of the crime scene at the Beale mansion, combined with autopsy results, failed to produce evidence sufficient to start much of an investigation. There are no fingerprints, trace evidence, murder weapon, or witnesses. Art suggests that he and Jack visit Beale's place of business, FA&O Shipping LLC, based at 501 Camp Street, in the heart of New Orleans's Lafayette Square. The square is within the Central Business District and was once the location for the Gallier Hall, the former city hall; for many years, it was the most popular spot to enjoy an assortment of jazz, blues and Zydeco music. The building is now a twelve-floor, mammoth, imposing structure.

As Jack and Art enter the building unannounced, they flash their badges at the security official who is covering the front security desk. Art authoritatively commands, "We need to speak to the CEO regarding an urgent matter."

The guard politely informs him that, "Mr. Blanchard, unfortunately, is away at a meeting in Washington, D.C. His business partner, Mr. Beale, has not yet arrived for work."

Art is insistent, "It is imperative that we speak with Mr. Blanchard over the phone, so who can provide us with his telephone number?"

The security official obeys, "I'll contact someone to help." He dials a four-digit number into the control panel of the phone on his desktop. Katherine Parchisi answers.

"Good morning Ms. Parchisi, this is Ronald at the front security desk. There are two police detectives here who want to speak to Mr. Blanchard or Mr. Beale. Mr. Blanchard is at a meeting in Washington, D.C., and Mr. Beale has not yet arrived this morning. They insist on contacting one of them via cell phone. What would you suggest I do?".

"Please hold a second, Ronald." After a couple of seconds, she tells him, "I'll send someone down to escort them to the seventh‑ floor main conference room. Please ask them to wait in the security lounge area until an escort arrives to pick them up."

Within minutes, a young man, appearing to be in his late twenties, arrives to serve as an escort for the two detectives.

Extending his hand for a shake, he greets them, "Good morning, Detectives, I'm David. I've been asked to escort you to the executive conference room. Please follow me. We'll take the executive elevator to save time."

They alight from the elevator thirty seconds later and Art and Jack follow David to the executive conference room. The room contains furniture from Cantoni's, one of the nation's leaders in modern furnishings and interior design, 3-d, Titan Zeus television monitors, and Spectrum Electric Motorized Projectors for viewing slides and film. FADFAY custom made European Luxury drapes shield the occupants from the harsh rays of the afternoon sun. In the center of the room is a twenty-five-foot long, mahogany conference table inspired by Frank Lloyd Wright's design style consisting of linear lines and the use of natural materials. The custom-made, oval-shaped table and the upholstered, chairs with thickly padded headrests comfortably accommodate at least eighteen people. David offers the detectives seats, "Someone will meet with you shortly," and then excuses himself.

Katherine Parchisi makes a grand entrance into the executive conference room from the set of beveled glass doors. Walking toward the detectives, who are now standing, she extends her right hand with a bright smile and says, "Good afternoon, I'm Katherine Parchisi, one of the legal partners. My department manages all of the legal affairs for FA&O Shipping LLC. I hope that I can assist you since Messrs. Beale and Blanchard are not available at the moment. If you're fine with that, how can I help you?"

Art starts first, "Well, I'm afraid we have some bad news for you."

Appearing unperturbed, Kathrine inquires, "And what might that be, Detective?"

"We understand that Mr. Beale was co-owner and chief legal counsel for the company?"

"That's correct, sir. Is there something wrong with Mr. Beale?" she asks, now looking nervous.

"I'm sorry to tell you that Mr. Beale was killed earlier today at his home."

"Oh no!" she shrieks in shock.

Tears stream from her eyes as she becomes noticeably unstable on her feet. The detectives quickly respond and approach her just in time to prevent injury as she nearly collapses on the thick carpet covering the floor. Her makeup is noticeably smeared under the wetness of her tears.

After a brief period of recovery, Ms. Parchisi apologizes for her sudden expression of shock and grief.

Art then consoles her and continues on with the business at hand, "If you're sufficiently recovered and willing to speak with us, we would like to ask you a few questions."

"I'm just so shocked! I'll rest later in my office suite, but I think I can manage to answer some of your questions, if it doesn't take too long."

"May we proceed then, Ms. Parchisi?"

"Yes, I think I can answer any questions you have, Detective."

"It is important that we get underway with our investigation as quickly as possible. The longer time and circumstances are on our side, the better our chances are of apprehending the individual responsible for Mr. Beale's death."

"Detective, if I may ask, exactly what happened to Mr. Beale?"

"Well, at this point in the investigation, I can only tell you that his body was discovered this morning, apparently killed in his mansion on Saint Charles Avenue." After letting that sink in, Art begins the questioning, "Ms. Parchisi, to the best of your knowledge, did Mr. Beale have any known enemies or anyone who would want to harm him?"

"Not that I'm aware of, Detective."

"Were there any ongoing business disputes with member-owners of the conglomerate?"

"Detective, in this multifaceted business, involving hundreds of millions of dollars annually, there are always business disputes, but nothing that I can think of that would rise to a level to justify killing Jason Beale."

"Were you aware of a scheduled a business meeting at Mr. Beal's home this morning?"

"No detective. I never heard of any business meeting being conducted at his home."

Art thanks her, then requests, "May we look at Mr. Beale's workspace?"

"Certainly, "I'm unaware of any privileged information that would be sitting out in the open for anyone's perusal. Please follow me."

Mr. Beale's workspace is a spacious and nicely appointed corner office, with a minimalistic, contemporary décor, overlooking Lafayette Square. An eight-foot-long conference table, surrounded by several plush black leather chairs, is situated on a Persian carpet as the room's centerpiece. The artwork, which consists of black and white images, gives the office an austere atmosphere.

As Jack surveys the office, he asks, "Ms. Parchisi is there a place in the office where Mr. Beale could secure money, valuables, or a weapon?"

"Not that I'm aware of. His desk is keyless, and probably only contains personal items and confidential business files. We'll cooperate with your investigation and honor any search warrant that you produce to fully access the contents of this office space."

"Thank you, Ms. Parchisi. Right now, we would appreciate your allowing us to review his personnel file for next of kin information. The department still has not contacted Mr. Beale's family."

"Yes, I think I can arrange that for you." She quickly makes a call, "This is Katherine Parchisi. Would you please bring Mr. Beale's personnel file to the seventh-floor executive conference room, right away...Thanks."

Five minutes later, one of the firm's secretaries brings the file to Katherine, She fans through the file and then spreads it out on the conference table to read, as the detectives hover over her shoulders. As she discovered after turning over page after page, there is no record of a next of kin or an alternate person to contact in the event of an urgent or emergency circumstance.

Art wraps up the meeting and tells Katherine, "You're an attorney, so you know how this works. We'll prepare a warrant for Mr. Beale's office space. As soon as the warrant is signed by the judge, we'll be back. Here are our business cards, we do appreciate your cooperation."

***

Both men are in deep thought as they depart the building and head to headquarters to update the Captain of detectives, Madelyn Grayson. The Captain is an old wily veteran who keeps very close tabs on the status of all major crimes in New Orleans. She is a forty-five-year-old African American who has been on the force for twenty-five years, the last seven of which she has held her current position. She attained her status on the strength of her intrinsic instincts, combined with her experience as a rank-and-file detective.

It is customary for Art and Jack to meet with the Captain in her office to update her on the status of all cases, especially heinous crimes such as the recent murder on Saint Charles Avenue. Madelyn often has suggestions for detectives about their respective cases, but everyone knows that a suggestion is an order. Failure to follow through with her suggested action could result in a stern tongue-lashing.

Once seated in the Captain's office containing a desk cluttered with papers, Art delivers his verbal status update. At that point, Madelyn suggests that he and Jack should consider a possible family connection to the murder. "Was Mr. Beale married?" to which Art replies, "To the best of our knowledge he's not married." "

That's interesting. All that money, a great job, a beautiful mansion with servants, and he doesn't have a wife? Tell me again, how old was this guy?"

Jack responded, "He was only fifty-one and we believe, based on the information we've gathered so far, that the guy was a loner."

Madelyn shakes her head. "There's something wrong with this picture, but I just can't seem to understand the incongruity. I suggest that you check on this as a possible crime of passion."

***

It is not business as usual at FA&O Shipping LLC, everyone is in shock when they are officially informed of Mr. Jason Beale's death. The case is being widely covered by the media. It is as if a funeral pall were cast over the building and its occupants.

Another person, not directly associated with the firm, who learned of the recent tragedy is Greg Pardee, a part-time longshoreman who works down at the New Orleans commercial shipping docks, where he unloads cargo from trucks, boats, or any other means of conveyance to earn a buck. When not involved in loading or unloading activities, Greg lives among the homeless community of New Orleans. Although the homeless population of New Orleans has dropped significantly from 11,600 in 2007 to 1,188 in 2018, Greg is not amongst those who have benefitted from the city's largesse in providing housing and social services for the indigent. Greg is in a bad way. Recently, his homeless status has worsened after a bunch of kids torched his tent containing all of his worldly possessions. Just bad, mean, and hateful kids with nothing more to do than harass homeless people. This is how teenagers go around having fun. Fortunately for Greg, he wasn't present when his tent was torched. Surely, he would have been killed.

Bad news generally spreads quickly in the world of commercial shipping, usually affecting truck drivers and longshoremen the most, and so is the case for Greg Pardee. He knows he has to figure out an angle to get enough money to hold him over until business picks up at the Port of New Orleans and he can reestablish his life as a homeless person.

Given Greg's homelessness and critical circumstances, Greg senses that there must be an angle he can exploit to secure sufficient money for living expenses in exchange for information. He is in dire need of money and is willing to do just about anything to get it, even if it means conniving, and weaving a tale of deceit.

Subsequently, the desk sergeant, posted at the front counter of police headquarters, answers the phone on the counter.

"Good morning," the caller says, "may I please speak with the cop in charge of homicide cases?"

"Do you mean Lieutenant Beauregard?"

"I'm sorry, but I don't know his name."

"I'll put you through, but what is your name and the nature of your call?"

"My name isn't important right now, but I might have information about a homicide case on Saint Charles Avenue."

"Hold on, please."

When the desk sergeant returns to the phone, he informs the caller, that "Lieutenant Beauregard is out of the office on another case. Would you like to leave a message for him?"

With a frustrated grunt, the caller hangs up. Given the recent publicity surrounding the gruesome crime on Saint Charles Avenue, the desk sergeant decides to draft a quick note about the call. He then places the note conspicuously on Art's desk.

CHAPTER FIVE

Taking Madelyn Grayson's suggestion, Art and Jack begin to pursue the case as a possible crime of passion. They sense that the best place to start is at the scene of the crime, on Saint Charles Avenue. Jack places a call to the Ivanov's. The phone rings several times without a response, so they decide to visit the couple.

When they arrive at the mansion, they see the crime scene tape still surrounding it. After there was no response to their knock at the front door, the detectives decide to make an unannounced visit to the rear of the property, where they are confronted by an eight-foot-high masonry wall. The wall is unclimbable. A metal gate guarding against entry onto the property incorporates a security panel requiring a dual digital code for entry.

As climbing over the eight-foot edifice or penetrating the security panel are both non-starters, once again, Jack dials the Ivanov's number, but to no avail. Puzzled, Jack asks rhetorically, "Could they have moved out of the premises that fast, and if so, why? We should check the phone service when we get back to the station."

The detectives know they need to conduct background checks on the Ivanov's because the couple has been nonresponsive to multiple phone calls. According to the telephone service carrier, the service is no longer in force. In light of the murder of their employer, suddenly terminating phone service is suspicious. Curious about the disappearance of the Ivanov couple, the detectives immediately conduct background checks, the result of which paints the profile of an average American married couple.

Background Assessment

Names: Dima and Nadia Ivanov

Citizenship: Both naturalized American citizens, in 2001

Ages: Mr. Ivanov, 49 and Mrs. Ivanov, 42

Address: 4701 Saint Charles Avenue

Ethnicity: White naturalized Americans, originating from the Russian nation

Telephone: 504-999-3510

Education: Unknown

Military: Unknown

Children: 1 son, Vladimir Jr, living in Russia, but not an American citizen

Banking: RT Federal Credit Union

Annual Income: $89,000 (Combined)

Prior work: Mr. Ivanov, nightclub bouncer while in Russia; Mrs. Ivanov, exotic dancer while in Russia

Convictions: Mr. Ivanov, 2 years served for assault with a deadly weapon

Next of Kin: None on file

"Art, the only thing outstanding on the background check is that Mr. Ivanov did a deuce for assault with a deadly weapon. There may be something to it."

Jack then adds, "Well, he was a bouncer in Russia, while she was a pole dancer. Whatever the case, we've got to find them, and quick."

"In the meantime," Art suggests, "to pursue the possible gay angle, we need to pull a picture of Mr. Beale from the DMV system, then start canvassing local gay business areas; we might find someone who recognizes our victim. Let's start in the gay area that runs along that stretch of St. Ann Street, near the heart of the French Quarter."

"Starting somewhere is better than starting nowhere," Jack chimes in.

Accompanied only by a picture of Mr. Beale and their combined determination, the two detectives head out to the area encompassing the St. Ann Street neighborhood, where gay life is dominant. The first business they approach is considered gay and gay-friendly. The assumption being that gay people, as well as anyone friendly to gay people, are welcome to join others in merriment and socialization.

The detectives split up upon entering the building. Jack ambles over to the bar, while Art takes a seat at an empty table. Jack motions to the bartender, withdraws a picture of Mr. Beale, and says to her, "Good evening." He flashes his badge. Now with the bartender's full attention, he says to her, "I'm Detective Sergeant Jack Fratelli, with the New Orleans Police Department. We're investigating a recent crime." He shows her the picture. "Have you ever seen this man?"

As she briefly studies the photo, she says, "No, I haven't."

Jack thanks her for speaking to him as, a man well over six feet tall approaches Art and asks if he can join him at the table, to which Art obliges, "Yes, of course."

As the man takes a seat, Jack waits a minute, then walks over to the table and asks if it is okay for him to join them. When the two seated men nod, Jack takes a seat.

The three men briefly share pleasantries and exchange handshakes. They engage in small talk about the New Orleans Saints football team. The taller man quips: "Some of those athletes are so muscular and powerful. They are just amazing in what they can do with their bodies." Art and Jack get his drift and continue to smile and listen attentively.

Finally, Jack says, "I'm looking for a friend of mine that I haven't seen since our days in the Navy, but I know that he lived in the Big Easy for a while. Would you guys mind taking a look at his picture to see if you might recognize him?"

Jack pulls out the picture of Mr. Beale from the breast pocket of his blazer and holds it up.

Art takes the picture in his hand and looks at it as if studying the image, then says, "No, never seen him." He offers the picture to the taller man, who takes it and looks closely. After a short period, he says, "I'm pretty sure I've seen a younger version of this guy over at Molly's Place."

Jack is excited about the information and wants more. "Do you remember the last time you saw him?"

"I only knew him by sight, but rumors float around this stretch of our neighborhood."

"Really? What rumors have you heard about him?"

"Well, if it's the same guy, the word is that he is rich, and has a distinct preference and interest in Russian men. I don't know if that's true or not, just a rumor."

"How many times would you say you've seen him in Molly's Place? Just asking because I wonder if it's worth checking over there."

"Oh, maybe four or five times."

Jack thanks the man for the information and says, "I miss him, and I've just got to find him." Then he leaves the table.

The taller man motions to Art and says, "Would you mind buying me a brewski?"

Art smiles. "No, I don't think so because my partner is waiting for me. He would never approve of me buying a drink for a complete stranger. He's the jealous type, you know what I mean?"

Art leaves the man sitting there in rejection and disappointment. Then he and Jack scurry to secure a search warrant.

***

A couple of hours later, now in possession of a search warrant for Mr. Beale's office space, Art and Jack are on their way to the corporate headquarters for FA&O

Shipping LLC. Upon their arrival, one of the firm's secretaries is waiting to escort them to Katherine Parchisi's suite of offices. As the men alight from the elevator, Katherine is standing there to greet them with a warm, but anticipatory smile. Once handshakes are executed, Art says, "Ms. Parchisi, as you know, we are here to execute a warrant on Mr. Beale's office workspace."

"Yes, gentlemen, I understand. Please follow me. Mr. Beale's office space was secured immediately after your last visit and no one has entered the office since that time."

She approaches the glass door to Mr. Beale's office space and then stops to enter a five-digit code into a wall-mounted security panel located adjacent to the glass entry door. An audible click sounds before the door quietly swings open to the inside. The detectives enter the room while Katherine remains posted just beyond the entrance. As trained, the detectives methodically search through desk drawers, file cabinets, large and small files, in between chair cushions, and even fanned pages of books and magazines in the hopes of finding anything unusual or that might assist with their investigation.

The only things of significance they find are several 8x10-inch head shots of men that could be characterized as "glamour photos." Each photo has a notation scribed on the back, which reads: "Best to Jason," followed by indiscernible writing, apparently intended as a signature. Art approaches the office door. "Ms. Parchisi, would you please step inside for a moment?" Katherine complies.

Art lays out the photos of the men on the conference table. "Have you ever seen any of these men before?" Katherine

"No, I haven't."

It might be a long shot, but Art and Jack decide to place the photos in sealed plastic envelopes and send them to the police lab for latent fingerprint analysis. They just might be able to derive the identities of the men featured in the photos. This might dovetail with their pursuit of the gay angle.

Art lets her know what they will be taking. "Ms. Parchisi, we also are seizing items as part of our search warrant, which includes an appointment book taken from Mr. Beale's desk drawer. We observed a couple of notations, apparently written a couple of days before Mr. Beale's death. As you can see here, one handwritten entry reads: 'Alan at 7:30 p.m.,' and another entry reads: 'Jeff at 11 a.m., angry.' Do you recognize either of these names?"

"Well, yes, Jason mentioned a famous writer, Alan Jared, but beyond that, I don't know him. I've never heard of this Jeff."

"Ms. Parchisi, thanks for your help. We'll be leaving now."

CHAPTER SIX

After returning to the squad bay that evening, tired, but determined, Jack conducts an Internet and DMV search for Alan Jared. He soon realizes that the subject of his search is a world-renowned author of several bestseller mystery novels. The sophisticated police database system that Jack uses in his search also reveals Alan's address. Armed with this information, Art and Jack decide to visit Alan at his home for questioning.

When they arrive at the address, Jack knocks on the door. As the door opens, the two detectives flash their badges, and Art introduces themselves "Sir, good afternoon, we're with the New Orleans Police Department. Is this the residence of Alan Jared?"

The very tall man says, "Yes, I'm Alan. How may I help you?"

"This is a private matter, sir. May we come in to talk?"

As the three men take seats in a beautiful living with a contemporary décor and simple, streamlined furnishings, Art gets right to the point. "We're investigating the death of Jason Beale. Did you know him?"

"Yes, I did, we were very close. I've been heartbroken since I heard about his death. He was very dear to me."

Jack probes further, "Do you know of anyone who may have wanted to hurt him, or with whom he may have had a serious dispute?"

"Well, several days ago, Jason told me about a previous relationship that he was on the verge of ending, but just wasn't sure how he wanted to go about it."

"Who might that have been, sir?".

"Well, Jason mentioned his name once. If memory serves me correctly, I believe it might have been Jeff."

"Do you know his last name?"

"No, I didn't retain the name because it didn't seem important then."

"Do you know if Mr. Beale was able to notify Jeff of his decision to break things off?"

"I'm not sure, but I know that he was fretful. He didn't want to meet with him in person and alone. He had toyed with the idea of sending him a letter advising him of his new love interest."

"And that new love interest would have been...?"

"Yes, Detective, I was that love interest."

"Mr. Jared, can you tell us where you were on the morning of February eleventh, at approximately eleven a.m.?"

"Are you asking me this because I'm a suspect in Jason's death?"

"Sir, at this point in our investigation, everyone is a suspect."

"Well, I consider your question as a personal insult, but in the spirit of cooperation, I'll answer. I was here, at home, drafting my latest novel. I usually start to work at about eight a.m. and I write until about one p.m."

"Sir, can anyone confirm that you were at home on that date and during those hours?"

"I can confirm that right away, but you are not to return to my home unless you have a search warrant signed by a duly appointed judge or magistrate." Alan pauses and calls out for his maid to come into the living room. "Maria, these two detectives want to ask you a question. Please answer them."

"Maria, were you here the morning of February eleventh with Mr. Jared?"

"Oh yes, Mr. Jared and I are here every morning." She pauses, then adds, "And on the eleventh we had lunch too. I work while he works on his stories."

When it is clear the detectives have no further questions, Alan quickly says, "Okay, thanks, Maria, that will be all. Please see these men to the front door."

As they reenter the squad car, Art mentions his assessment of the meeting with Alan. "I think he was insulted by our questions, but we just came up with another possible suspect. We need to do a background check on this guy Jeff, but we need a last name."

After thinking for a moment, Art concludes, "If this guy Jeff was sweet on Jason, they probably talked a fair number of times on the phone, so let's get copies of Jason Beale's telephone bills and try to ID Jeff that way."

With some delay and effort, Art and Jack determine Jeff's last name and address. Art suggests, "Before we knock on Jeff's door, let's complete his background check so we know who we're talking to."

The two detectives are anxious to review the background assessment for Jeff Gaskins.

Background Assessment

Name:	Jeff Gaskins
Address:	123 Lotus Place
Telephone:	504-123-0045
Age:	37
Marital:	Single
Citizenship:	American
Ethnicity:	Caucasian
Education:	Graduate of Calvin Coolidge HS
Employment:	Unknown
Income:	Unknown
Banking:	Unknown
Convictions:	1) Petty theft, 2) assault, and 3) indecent exposure. Time served: probation and fines
Hobbies:	Bodybuilder

After reading, Jack gives his opinion of Jeff. "If I didn't know any better, I'd say this guy might be a bum. Maybe he's down on his luck and lives with his parents."

Art stresses what is most important. "But more significant is this: What is Jeff's relationship with Mr. Beale? I guess we'll find out. Let's ride."

The unassuming house at 123 Lotus Place is situated in a middle-class neighborhood. The house seems to be well maintained. Jack knocks and aa moment later, a woman of average height stands there with a quizzical look on her face. Her features suggest she may be of Mediterranean descent.

"Are you from the police?"

Art politely affirms "Yes, ma'am, we are."

"Oh, my goodness," she shrieks, "is Jeff in trouble again?"

Jack did not want to divulge too much at this point. "Well, we're not sure of that, ma'am. We just need to speak to him. Does he live here?"

"Yes, he does, sometimes."

"Is he at home right now?"

"Yes, he's upstairs sleeping. His father is here too. Would you like to speak with him also?"

"No, ma'am, just Jeff."

Mrs. Gaskins says she's too old to walk up and down the stairs, so she yells out to call Jeff downstairs. There's no response.

"Would you mind going up and knocking on his door, second on the left?" she asks the detectives.

Art was glad to have her permission to investigate further. "Of course, we will with your permission."

Once arriving at the top of the stairs and standing at Jeff's bedroom door, Jack knocks and says, "Police," but there's no response. Jack then cautiously twists the door handle and starts to enter. "This is the police, we're coming in."

Art carefully unholsters his service revolver because of the potential danger; the suspect could be their man. As they peer into the darkened room, they see the large figure of a man who seems to be sleeping. Jack gives Jeff a couple of gentle nudges, resulting in his awakening.

Jeff was startled. "What the fuck! Who the fuck are you?"

Jack wanted to quickly clarify who they were. "We're cops. Your mother asked us to wake you up."

"So, what the fuck do you want, man?"

"We want to ask you some questions about your friend Jason Beale. Was Jason Beale angry with you for some reason?"

After realizing what is going on, Jeff stands up, towering over Art and Jack. "Look, cops, my lawyers have always told me to never talk to a cop or answer questions, so I don't want to answer your questions. "Now, get out of my house," he thundered. I won't tell you again he said, threateningly. Get out," he yelled, "Hey, Mom, I want these jokers out of my room!"

Honoring Jeff's right not to answer questions, Art and Jack reluctantly leave the premises. Once outside the house, Jack is satisfied that Jeff is their man. "I like him as a suspect, and he fits our height profile."

"Yeah Jack, but that's a flimsy justification for interviewing him about his personal or business relationship with Jason Beale."

Jack is adamant that he is right. "This guy seems to be financially destitute, so I don't think there was a business relationship between them. Living with his parents at age thirty-seven, and no discernible means of income? He's a mama's boy. That only leaves a close and personal relationship as the reason for them to know one another. We've got to find a way to get him to talk to us."

"Okay, Jack, but let's get on to our next objective, exploring the gay life area and seeing if anyone can identify our glamour photo. The best place to start is Molly's place."

***

Molly's Place, located along a quaint stretch of St. Ann Street, is the "go-to" upscale bar and eatery that has a large gay clientele. This bustling spot features an eclectic menu consisting of the most popular dish of buffalo meat sliders, served alongside guacamole and cheese fries. Most enticing for the regulars who can always be found there at least 4 times a week, are the 20 varieties of wine, beer and dark ales. Many close friendships are known to have been formed while dining at Molly's Place, where the atmosphere is warm, friendly, and inviting.

An attractive young female in her mid-twenties is waiting tables as Art walks through the front door. As he surveys the room, he waits to be seated. Soon a greeter escorts him to a table occupied by an elderly couple.

"I don't mean to intrude or create an uncomfortable dining experience for you. Do you mind?"

The male customer really didn't want any company during his meal, but was polite any way. "Please join us."

"Thanks, I'm waiting for my partner, who should be arriving shortly."

Jack enters the bar and is immediately greeted by the waitress, who seems to be in a rush. "Hello, I'm looking for an old friend who I've been told comes here." He pulls Mr. Beale's picture from his coat pocket, and as he shows it to her he says, "Do you know this guy or have you ever seen him around here?"

After studying the picture for several seconds, the waitress says, "No, sorry, I can't help you." And then she is scurries away in a rush.

As Jack looks around the bar, he sees open seats are running short. The greeter recognizes the situation and offers to seat Jack at the table where Art is seated and talking to the elderly couple. Once seated and settled in, Jack introduces himself as a detective with the New Orleans Police Department, and remarks that he is looking for someone who is frequently seen in the bar.

Jack shows the picture to everyone seated at the table. "Have you ever seen the man in this photo?"

Art and the elderly man shake their heads and sternly grumble "No." The elderly woman, however, is willing to talk. "I think I've seen a guy that resembles him, but he may have been a bit older. It seems like I've seen him someplace other than this place, but I just can't put my finger on it."

The waitress is taking food orders at a nearby table and she overhears the conversation about the picture. As she approaches Jack's table to take their orders, she motions toward the counter and explains, "The owner of the bar has been forced to tend bar tonight because the main bartender called in sick. Since he knows just about everybody that comes in here, you might want to ask him about your picture."

Jack stands and politely excuses himself before heading over to the bar. He waits there only a few seconds before the bar owner says, "What can I get you?"

Jack produces the photo and says, "I just need some information. Do you know this man or have you ever seen him here, or in any other place, before?"

The bar owner looks at the photo. "Are you some kind of a cop?"

Jack flashes his badge. "Yes, I'm with the New Orleans Police Department."

The bar owner looks Jack in his eyes and smiles. "Thanks for visiting my place, but no, I don't know him."

"And you've never seen him here in the bar?" Jack counters.

"Sorry I can't help you, officer, but you might want to try one of the other eateries in the area."

Jack and Art continue to canvass businesses along St. Ann Street until the usual closing times, between 12:30 and 2 a.m. Art decides to call it a night, but wants to summarize events for his daily report. "We visited eleven bars and restaurants and interviewed at least a dozen people who were either customers, waitstaff, or owners."

"The most promising information we gathered was from the elderly lady at Molly's Place and before that, the tall guy who asked you to buy him a brewski," Jack adds. "That's not much to go on."

"You know Art, that bar owner, behind the counter at Molly's Place? I think he was lying to me."

"What makes you say that?"

"Nothing more than cop instincts. First thing in the morning, let's run a background check on him."

CHAPTER SEVEN

As Art and Jack approach Captain Grayson's office, they knew they had not made much progress on the case, and needed to do something to tie things up. Art was pondering different strategies in his mind, "Maybe we could keep an eye on the suspect by putting a GPA tracker on his car and follow him around, or have him surveilled by a police helicopter. "Art, puts his thoughts aside as they enter Captain Grayson's office.

She beckons them in with a wave of her hand and a warm smile. "Please take a seat. I know that you've turned in your daily after-action report, but tell me about the progress you've made on the case involving the murder on Saint Charles Avenue. There's already a lot of pressure coming from the Mayor's office about this case. Let me frame this for you, gentlemen: Mr. Beale was on the Mayor's list of elite donors to his reelection campaign. The Mayor called the Chief this morning and had a few strong words of encouragement to find the killer of his friend Mr. Beale. The Chief then called me to say that you guys were out late yesterday and visited several bars in the St. Ann Street neighborhood, showing photos and asking questions."

Art interjects, "That's right, Captain. We're following standard protocols of investigation."

"I suppose you were in the neighborhood because of the gay angle that I suggested, correct?"

"Yes, Captain, that's right, but what we found out was far less than earthshaking. I'd like to continue, if I might?"

"Please do so, Lieutenant. You have my full and undivided attention."

"We have two people who believe they've seen a younger version of the man in the photo we showed around the neighborhood. We also believe the bar owner at Molly's Place was lying when he failed to recognize the photo of Mr. Beale.

"We're currently in the process of conducting a background check on the bar owner. That should be completed by midday today. Additionally, we had the lab run forensics on photos of men taken as part of our search warrant at Mr. Beale's office. We're hoping latent fingerprints might be produced, leading to the identity of the men. Of course, we'd like to speak to them. There could be a murder motive behind the photos. We need to know why he had glamour photos of men wedged away in a corner of his desk. Hardly incriminating, but we also discovered an appointment book in Mr. Beale's office desk. There were two handwritten notes involving the names of two men: Alan and Jeff. Both fit within the height profile provided by a neighbor who saw such a man walking in the neighborhood on the day of Mr. Beale's death. This guy, Jeff Gaskins, we like him a lot as a suspect. We haven't made a connection yet, but we're investigating to determine the reason for those entries.

We suspect Mr. Beale may have been hiding something as a result having, such as a gay lifestyle. We also believe our suspect to be taller than average with a tan complexion; he could be Hispanic, African American, or maybe even of Mediterranean descent.

Finally, as far as we know, it doesn't appear that the murder was motivated by burglary. That's because there was no indication that items of real value were missing from the mansion. We might know more after contacting the Ivanov couple, but their telephone service has been turned off and they seem to have absconded. We want answers to both of those issues."

Captain Grayson was pleasantly surprised that the detectives had at least some significant leads to follow up on. "Okay, Detectives, thanks for the update."

In the form of a question, and in her special way, the Captain suggests that there might be a foreign interest or angle to the case. Art and Jack know exactly what that means…follow her suggestion.

As Art arrives at his desk, he notices a yellow sticky wedged slightly under the green ink blotter covering his desk. It states:

"Unknown male caller wanted to speak to you while you were out of office. The caller said he had information about the Saint Charles Avenue murder, but refused to leave his name."

The note was signed by Desk Sergeant Max Redman.

Art immediately grabs the phone and dials the front desk.

"Hello, this is Sergeant Thomas. How may I help you, sir?"

"Sergeant, this is Lieutenant Beauregard in homicide. What is Sergeant Redman's twenty?"

"He's not on duty today, Lieutenant. He won't be back on duty until tomorrow."

"We need to speak with him right away. Can you get him on the line?"

"I'll try, sir."

In the meantime, Art shares the news and possible lead on the murder case with Jack.

Two minutes later, Sergeant Redman is on the phone with Art, who thanks him for promptly calling back.

"I'm going to place the call on speakerphone." Art leans outside his office door and motions Jack to come in. "My partner, Sergeant Jack Fratelli, is here listening to our conversation. Is that okay with you?"

"Yes, sir, that's okay."

"You left an interesting note on my desk about a caller claiming to have information about the recent murder on Saint Charles Avenue."

"Yes, sir, I remember leaving the note."

"The content of your note, coming from the caller, has generated several questions that I hope you're able to answer."

"I'll try my best, sir."

"Did the man speak clearly or did he have an accent?"

"Sir, he seemed to be English fluent, without a noticeable accent."

"Did he sound young or old?"

"My guess is that he was between thirty and forty."

"Did he sound more like a professional type of man?"

"From what I could deduce from our short conversation, he was an average dude, sir. I didn't detect any polish in his speech."

"Did he sound sincere and convincing?"

"Sir, the reason that I left the note for you was because I found no reason to believe it was a bullshit call. He was real."

"Can you tell me anything else about the call?"

"Well, I believe the caller was standing outside at the time of the call because of the background noise."

"What did you hear in the background?"

"It sounded like loud vehicles and some sort of churning sound as they motored along, Lieutenant. I think I also heard a clanking sound, like a bell ringing on a boat."

"Okay, I've overlooked maybe the most important thing. Why did the man refuse to leave his name?"

"I don't know, Lieutenant. He said he had information about the Saint Charles Avenue murder. When I asked for his name, he refused to give it, so I placed the call on hold and attempted to connect him to your office telephone, but there was no answer. When I came back to the caller's phone line, he was gone."

Art again thanks the sergeant for responding so quickly while on his day off. "Jack, we've got to find this anonymous dude. He could be the lynchpin to solving this case. Max mentioned a clanking sound and a possible sound of a bell, maybe coming from a boat. Combining those sounds with the shipping business that our victim was involved in could potentially provide us with a lead to explore in this case."

Art and Jack simultaneously review an expedited official background check on the owner of Molly's Place:

Background Assessment

Name:	Julius Raymond
Address:	1437 Eighth Street
Home Value:	$1,800,000
Telephone:	985-177-0963
Convictions:	3 years served for illegal smuggling; 1 year served for assault with a deadly weapon
Aliases:	Jimmy Breeze
Ethnicity:	White, Russian-American, naturalized citizen
Military:	Unreported
Education:	12 years, Russia
Profession:	Restaurateur
Banking:	RT Federal Credit Union
Annual Personal Income:	$109,100
Driver's license:	Louisiana, N7097496
Marital:	Spouse, Gregory Raymond
Vehicles:	Mercedes Benz SL 550; BMW M760i
Parents:	Deceased

Jack thought the assessment revealed something odd. "Art, do you that is it normal for a restaurateur earning a hundred grand personal income to control such wealth that includes a home valued at nearly two million bucks, along with a two-hundred-thousand-dollar BMW and a Mercedes Benz SL 550 valued in excess of a hundred thirty-five grand?"

I'm wondering the same thing, Jack. To maintain that type of lifestyle, he can't possibly be getting all of his money out of Molly's Place. His previous conviction is starting to cast an aspersion over this guy. Looking at it another way, he might have sufficient income to sustain that lifestyle if his spouse has income as well. There might even be some kind of inheritance or earnings from gambling that justifies the material things noted in the background check."

"Yeah, I agree with you, the report doesn't show income generated by his spouse, Gregory. I'd like to know more about Gregory and if he has an income. We'll just have to keep this guy in mind as we proceed with our investigation, remembering that he lied to us and could be an important piece to our investigation. This guy is dirty; he served three years in the penitentiary and appears to be living beyond his means. Let's ask Gregory about his employment when we visit him for an interview."

"Let's call it a day and try to get a couple hours of sleep before hitting the pavement tomorrow."

***

Another morning arrives and the detectives have few clues to work on as they work under pressure to solve the murder, that is until a male caller dials the phone number to the Headquarters building for the New Orleans Police

Department. Desk Sergeant Redman answers the call, and identifies himself, "How may I help you?"

"I would like to talk to the cop investigating the murder of the rich guy over on Saint Charles Avenue."

"Sir, before transferring your call, may I have your name?"

"Yes, for now, I'm Mary."

Sergeant Redman says, "Please hold, sir, you'll be connected momentarily."

Art accepts the call after Sergeant Redman quickly briefs him about the nature of the conversation so far. Art answers the phone by identifying himself and says, "Good morning, how can I be of assistance?"

"I've been trying to get ahold of you about the murder of that rich guy over in the Garden District. Is there a reward being offered for information, because I need money?"

Art is listening very closely to the caller's voice characteristics and background noise. He mentally notes the sound of a bell and what sounds like a foghorn going off.

"So, tell me, what do you know about the case?"

"I know enough, Detective, but you haven't answered my question yet."

"Well. No, there's no reward at this time, but I might be able to swing something."

"What does that mean?"

"Well, if you're ever in trouble down on the docks at the Port, you can call me to see if I can help you out."

If the caller is surprised that Art appears to know where he's calling from, he doesn't show it. Instead, he responds, "That's not good enough, Mr. Detective. I'll call again in a couple of days to see if any money is available for my information."

Sensing the caller is about to hang up, Art blurts out, "Just a minute—" but before he can complete his sentence, the caller hangs up and the line goes silent.

CHAPTER EIGHT

After another day of chasing down witnesses and searching for clues, Art takes a deep breath while going to drop off his daily after-action report. As Captain Grayson walks back into her office, she questions him about his progress in uncovering more evidence. He briefs her on the background check developed for the bar owner of Molly's Place.

"Well, Art, why do you believe the guy lied to you?"

"It's mainly based on cop instincts resulting from his apparent nervousness and subtle mannerisms observed during the interview."

Art also mentions that a man called who claimed to have information about Jason Beale's murder, but refused to leave his name.

"That all sounds interesting and a bit intriguing." She picks up his report and begins fanning through it as she looks at him through the corner of her eye. "Given what little you have, you might as well check to see if there's any bad blood between Mr. Beale and the minority owners. Besides, who will benefit the most from Mr. Beale's demise? What about that guy, Blanchard, who was out of town when you first visited his company? Sometimes a partnership can sour because of jealousy, anger, greed, or reasons that simply defy logic, resulting in the demise of a business or personal relationship."

***

Since Kenneth Blanchard might be back from his business trip to Washington, D.C. by now, Art and Jack follow the Captain's suggestion. The two detectives arrange a meeting to interview the surviving majority partner.

Kenneth Blanchard is a handsome, bald African American, who appears to have retained his tall, slender, and muscular physique from his days as a quarter back with the New Orleans Saints football team. He appears to be about forty-five years of age, articulate, and well spoken. He greets the detectives warmly as they alight from the executive elevator.

Handshakes are executed, and the detectives follow Mr. Blanchard into his office suite. The office décor is reflective of its occupant with pictures of Blanchard in his football uniform and sports memorabilia prominently displayed.

"So, Detectives, please be seated at the conference table. Ms. Parchisi briefed me earlier regarding Jason's death and the execution of your search warrant for Jason's office workspace. By the way, can I offer you tea or coffee? I even have beignets"

Art is taken aback at his social graces, so untypical for a jock. "Thanks, but no, sir. We'd like to get right to the reason for our visit if you don't mind?"

Blanchard nods his head affirmatively and gestures with his hands to proceed with the questioning.

Art begins the informal interrogation, "You may have been closest to Mr. Beale as his business partner. Did you both own equal parts of the company?"

"Actually, no. I retained fifty-five percent ownership, while Jason controlled thirty percent. The remaining fifteen percent is controlled by several minority owners."

Art pushes for him to elaborate: "I assume all of that is spelled out in your partnership agreement?"

"Absolutely, and in fairly gross detail."

"Mr. Blanchard, do you know of any men working in the building who wear a gray fedora?"

Blanchard thinks for a moment before responding, "No, Detective, I'm afraid not."

"We discovered the names of two men in Mr. Beale's appointment book."

"Yes, Detective, I'm aware of that."

"The names we found were Alan and Jeff. Are you familiar with either of those names?"

"No, I'm afraid not."

"It's our understanding that Mr. Beale may have been married. Is that correct?" Art is trying to determine if Mr. Blanchard would lie.

"Not that I'm aware of, Detective. As far as I knew, he enjoyed his life as a single guy."

"Upon execution of our search warrant, we retained several eight-by-ten photographs of men that were wedged in a corner of Mr. Beale's desk. That may be meaningless, but do you know anything about the photos or if Mr. Beale was possibly gay?"

"I'm afraid not, gentlemen."

"How would you describe your relationship with Mr. Beale?".

"It was always businesslike, and we celebrated our goals and objectives as they occurred."

"Mr. Blanchard, just one more thing: Can you tell us where you were on the morning of Tuesday, February sixteenth?"

"I was in Washington, D.C. on business."

"Can you tell us where you stayed while there?"

"Gentlemen, this is getting into the realm of personal privacy. I don't know anything about this, nor did I ever pry into Jason's personal life. I have not committed a crime, as I sense you might suspect, neither am I obligated to continue this interrogation. Now, if you'll please excuse me, I have a busy schedule today. You'll be escorted out of the building. Good day, gentlemen!"

They hurry back to the squad car to discuss what they've just uncovered. Jack, "Did we just strike a sensitive nerve with him?"

"It looks and sounds like we did. I like him. Now, what should we do next?."

"I've got it Jack, since we've been to the top of the business chain and didn't reap much from our effort, we might as well assess the bottom,"

"Are you talking about the docks at the Port of New Orleans?"

"Well, that's where goods are loaded into or unloaded from commercial ships. I've done some initial research and gathered this information: There are approximately twelve hundred men and women that work as longshoremen along the docks of the Port of New Orleans. Longshoremen working at the port are represented by four unions. That makes for a large workforce serving a single discrete industry."

They go to the employment office at the Port of New Orleans to inquire about the hiring process and determine if work is available. As they arrive, they observe many men sitting on benches lining the walls in the room. Even the wooden chairs in the center of the room are occupied by job seekers. They decide to stand with the other men without a place to sit.

Art and Jack know that anything affecting FA&O Shipping LLC ultimately affects dock operations at the Port. They concede that visiting the Port of New Orleans is a long shot, but they are hoping to hear about anything that might signal information regarding the murder.

The conversational chatter in the room amongst the job seekers is fairly loud. Art extends a hand to the man standing next to him, who identifies himself as James. They give each other a firm handshake. Art leans over toward James and asks about the hiring process and if he thinks everyone will get called for work today. James explains that work has been slow since the killing of one of the big bosses, but he doesn't know why. James mentions, however, that there has been widespread gossip about "one of the big bosses being gay" and that his lover may have worked in the corporate office.

Acting a bit coy, Art smiles inappropriately and asks Jim if he knows the dude's name.

James says: "You mean the lover?"

"Yeah."

"Nah, never heard it. Man, it might not even be true. Sometimes these guys down here on the docks make up stuff just for the hell of it. It's probably just a rumor."

After engaging in further small talk with the job seekers, Art and Jack depart the Port. As the men walk to their undercover police cruiser, Art hears a clanking sound and bells ringing. He's certain that the sounds are the same as or similar to what he heard during his conversation with the mysterious anonymous caller, the one who demanded money for information.

CHAPTER NINE

A middle-aged woman is 743 miles away from New Orleans, ensconced at the Port of Charleston, where she and her business partner live in a newly purchased luxury houseboat. Even though it was financed with a huge interest rate, the owners were desperate to get the two-story vessel to use to complete their mission. Cautiously, one of the female occupants views the outside area from an interior porthole, looking for intruders or any unusual or unsafe conditions. Satisfied that all is well, she is relieved by news of the scheduled delivery, after which she and her husband can disappear forever into retirement. She's not yet fully acclimated to her new home and the general environment because she's never before lived under such cramped conditions. Her attitude at this point is that she has a business requiring her undivided attention, so for now, she'll put up with the situation. Later, she and her business partner will relocate to a place where there is no extradition treaty with the United States. Such has always been a prominent component of their life and business plan. This would entail living out their lives in luxury and obscurity.

The woman sits down at a table in front of a bank of personal computers that are ready to execute the commands produced by her fingertips. Unexpectedly, one of the computer screens starts to blink rapidly. She recognizes this to be a potentially urgent message, requiring her immediate attention and response. She confirms its authenticity as an encrypted electronic message that she should act on urgently.

She depresses an encryption button and enters into the keyboard a secret six-digit code, resulting in a discernable message that reads: "250 were ordered and scheduled for delivery in 5 days, valued at $1,500,000."

The woman sends an encrypted return message, confirming receipt of the message. Also confirmed is the planned time and place for cargo delivery and pickup. This will be the third and final shipment scheduled for this month. She's delighted by the news and confident that all will go well because, over the last several years, there have been so many of the very same type of deliveries.

She and her partner continue to acquire significant wealth from their business venture. Since the stress associated with delivery of the order has dissipated, she feels as if she can now relax. As a result, the woman realizes that she's tired and a bit hungry, so she starts to prepare dinner for herself and her business partner. Just as the scent of tomatoes and garlic begins to infuse the interior of the boat cabin, Dima Ivanov steps onto the main deck and grabs his wife around her waist. He tells her he's hungry as he stretches his arms wide to eliminate tightness from napping all afternoon in the lower berth.

Nadia Ivanov says to her husband, "Earlier this afternoon, I received the electronic message we were expecting. It confirmed cargo delivery in five days at the usual time and location. In accordance with our standard protocols, trucks, drivers, and a few extra men will be in place to help load and distribute the precious cargo to predetermined points along the eastern seaboard."

"That's great, but have you heard anything from the connection?"

"No, nothing yet."

"Okay, we'll just continue to lay low until things cool off and those two goon detectives have no other choice than to turn this into a cold case. By then, we'll be long gone to our retirement destination."

"Yes, but I'm very worried about Mr. Beale's murder. We were very quiet and kept a low profile, so I just can't figure out how Mr. Beale found out about our operations from the grounds of the mansion."

"That's not that important right now because we'll soon be out of here and living the good life and rolling in dough! Riley."

"I guess you're right, honey." She smiles and raises her voice for emphasis. "The cargo is perishable, so we must make certain that the correct environmental conditions are maintained for the long journey along the east coast and onward."

***

The Ivanovs are not the only ones with ties to the connection. Julius Raymond has worked many years for the connection as an operative in the lucrative business of smuggling cargo into the United States. The connection places a telephone call to Julius Raymond through a throwaway cellular phone. Secret and encrypted communications are one of the absolutes in the business of illegal smuggling. As the connection speaks into the phone, he emphasizes secrecy and directs Julius to meet him in the French Quarter tonight at 9 p.m., on Bourbon Street at the crossing of St. Peter Street.

As discussed earlier in the day, the two men meet that night, as planned. "How did you come to learn about Beale's love affair?" the connection inquired.

"I always suspected he was gay, so six months ago, I arranged for him to meet a couple of very cute guys. I was able to develop good information about their relationship."

"What type of information are you talking about?"

"Sex. What else is there in the life of gay men? He was head-over-heels infatuated with one of the guys that I set him up with. They dated multiple times, often meeting for food and drinks at my place on St. Ann Street."

"You mean your bar?"

"Yes, and as a gift, his new lover gave him an eight-by-ten glossy glamour photo of himself as a demonstration of his affection. What's more, a video session is available. This, of course, is all part of doing business."

The connection counters, "Do you mean to tell me you're in possession of intimate videotapes of Jason Beale?"

"Yes," Julius affirms, smiling broadly.

"If either of them show-up together in the bar again, let me know. I need to keep very close tabs on this situation."

The next evening, the connection places another call to Julius. Once he answers the phone, Julius lets him know he is worried, "I'm getting nervous because a cop was in the bar last night, flashing his badge and showing a picture of Jason Beale. He wanted to know if I recognized Beale. Of course, I said no. Where there's one cop, there are many."

The connection abruptly interrupts Julius's nervous chatter and tells him to calm down, and that he doesn't want to discuss anything over the phone. He tries to placate Julius. "Your bar was probably one of several places the cop visited." The connection realizes that if the cops are suspicious of Julius, he might be next, which would be an intolerable situation.

"Julius, you know that cops always take a wide-view approach to any investigation. They probably don't have sufficient reason to believe you are a suspect in Beale's death. So just calm down. Meet me tonight in the Quarter, at the usual place, where we can melt into the crowd. We won't be noticed. Since the cops probably have you on their radar, make sure you're not followed and don't tell anyone about our meeting. I want to hear the entire story from last night, in detail."

The two men arrive at their planned location at about the same time. Bourbon Street is busy as usual with many people milling around carrying open bottles of beer. The strong scent of marijuana waifs through the crowds in the evening air.

"Thanks, Julius, for coming out and meeting with me tonight. I believe Jason may have reported the business to the cops. The only leverages we had over Beale are the photos and a couple of videotaped sex sessions. But that probably wasn't enough to stop him from going to the cops. Now, please tell me exactly what happened last night. I need the details."

Julius lays out a detailed account of previous evening's events. "Sir, I was so nervous after the cop left the bar, I had to snort some cocaine to help me calm down. I was almost ready to piss in my pants."

As Julius finishes explaining what happened at his bar last night, the connection listens intently. They walk slowly, proceeding east on St. Peter Street where the lighting is poor and obscures their facial features. Given the sensitivity of the situation and the subject, privacy is essential.

"Let's be clear, Julius. I understand that Mr. Beale had to be eliminated because he found out about the business we were conducting from the rear of his home."

As they continue to talk while standing in the shadows, the connection unwraps a long cigar. "Okay, Julius, thanks for coming and describing the events of last night. Oh, and by the way, for notifying me, there's a large cash bonus for you tonight."

"Thanks, sir."

The connection smiled cooingly. "Now Julius, what you've said is all very interesting, but we can easily handle things as small as this. I need to light my cigar, but I must've left my lighter at home. Do you have a light on you?"

As Julius rummages through his front and back pockets with both hands, he is caught off guard when suddenly and without warning, the connection withdraws a long-bladed knife and quickly plunges it into Julius's chest, puncturing a lung. Immediately, Julius collapses to the ground and desperately gasps for air. While he's incapacitated, the connection inflicts a *coup de grâce* horizontally across his exposed neck, severing his jugular vein. The two swift knife blows take less than ten seconds. The connection is without conscious and has no shame or guilt about his nefarious activities.

Julius dies on that very spot, and the connection slithers away in the darkness of the night. The connection knew that he had no other choice than to kill Julius because he was unstable, talked too much, and was as loose as the chairs on the deck of the *Titan*

CHAPTER TEN

Feeling confident that they are close to cracking the case, Art and Jack try to tie up loose ends. "Jack, I'm still bothered by that guy Raymond. He lied to me about the photo I showed him last night. His response to my questions gave off some distinct negative vibes. And my cop instincts told me that he was very nervous, especially after I flashed my badge on him. I think we owe him another visit, especially because one of his convictions was for assault with a deadly weapon."

"I totally agree, let's ride. At this hour of the day, the bar should be filled with other customers who might recognize Mr. Beale's picture."

As they enter the bar, the greeter intercepts the detectives.

"Good evening, would you like to be seated?"

Art returns the greeting and politely asks the waitress if the owner is available.

"No, I'm sorry, he's on an errand at the moment. He should be back soon."

"Okay, thanks, is it okay if we just have a couple of soft drinks over at the bar while we wait?"

"Of course, just give him a few minutes."

As they sit waiting, Jack grabs at the inside pocket of his sports coat and pulls out his cell phone, which is vibrating silently.

"Hello, this is Detective Fratelli, badge 763."

"Sir, this is dispatch. There is a 187 at the corner of Bourbon Street and St. Peter Street. You seem to be the unit nearest that location."

"Affirmative, we can be on scene within three to five minutes."

Jack and Art depart the bar in a rush, and about three minutes later, they arrive at the scene of a gruesome homicide.

Two patrolmen are on the scene, warding back gawkers. Jack approaches the patrolmen. "What happened here?"

"This is how he was found, sir, apparently stabbed in the chest. His throat appears to have been slashed as well. From the looks of it, the laceration across his neck is very deep and was probably the fatal blow."

"Are there any witnesses?".

"None that we can determine at this point, sir. This area is usually dark."

"Does he have any ID?" Art inquires.

"Yes sir, here's his wallet with his driver's license."

As Art pries open the wallet, he is taken aback by the name on the driver's license: Julius Raymond. Somberly, Art hands the wallet with the license to Jack for confirmation.

"Art, this might be linked to the Beale case." The coroner arrives and confirms the two deadly wounds observed by the detectives as the probable cause of death.

In the event of the death of a citizen, departmental regulations require a police officer to contact the decedent's next of kin for death notification. This is a task that most officers dread performing. Art and Jack arrive at 1437 Eighth Street, the address of record for Julius Raymond. A knock on the front door of the residence is answered through a speaker, by what seems to be the voice of a female.

"How may I help you?"

Art is anxious to get on with the formalities and get down to business. "We are with the New Orleans Police Department and would like to speak to you about an important matter."

"Well, what is it?"

"Ma'am, we need to speak with you privately. I assure you it should only take a few minutes of your time."

"Okay, hold on a minute, I'm cooking a late dinner for my husband."

After a couple of minutes, the door opens and there stands a man over six feet in height. He's wearing an apron, flip-flops, and undershirt while holding a large metal spoon in his hand. His cheeks are slightly reddened by what appears to be rouge. Art and Jack, who are frozen with shock, flash their badges. Jack manages to summon enough composure to talk without showing that he has been surprised by the man's appearance. "We're sorry to disturb you, but we have urgent information. Is this the residence of Julius Raymond and are you his next of kin?"

"I'm Gregory, and yes, Julius lives here. We've been married for five years. Why, what is this about?"

"May we please step inside to talk?"

Gregory holds the door open and beckons them inside, where they take seats. Jack is perplexed by what he has just heard. "Do you and Julius work together at his place of business?"

"No, I don't work, I'm a stay-at-home wife."

"Can you tell us the last time you saw Julius?"

"It was earlier this evening, about seven p.m. Is Julius okay?"

Jack breaks the bad news. "No, I'm sorry to inform you that Julius was killed earlier tonight."

"You can't be serious!" Gregory shrills, as copious tears begin to stream down his face. After he has been crying for a couple of minutes, Art and Jack offer to arrange for medical ambulance support. Their attempts to soothe Gregory with sympathetic words are without effect. They provide Gregory with business cards for the medical examiner's office to make arrangements for the release of Raymond's body. Overcome with grief, Gregory continues to cry as Art and Jack leave the premises.

The next morning, Art and Jack brief Captain Grayson on the death of Julius Raymond and the rumors that are developing on the docks regarding Beale's death. They further explain their hunch that a possible link exists between the two deaths and that they will be steadfast in their efforts to find out the facts.

"What have you found out about the Ivanov couple? Where are they? Why would they disappear so quickly after their employer is found brutally murdered? And what about the possible fingerprints from the photos of those men?" Finally, she barks out, "Get some answers! The chief is all over my rear end about this case!"

Art checks in with the coroner's office to confirm the cause of death for Julius Raymond and Jason Beale. The coroner, whom Art has known for many years, is named Peter Henery.

"Well, Art, Julius Raymond's death resulted from a massive laceration to the left side of the neck, causing rapid and voluminous blood loss, combined with near decapitation. Contributing to his death was an open pneumothorax, better known as a puncture wound to the left lung, accompanied by significant pain, massive hemorrhaging, and limited ability to breathe. Oh, and by the way, we detected an unknown blood source on the body, the contributor of which is unknown, but we're running a DNA analysis.

"Julius Raymond's wounds were deep, resulting in massive trauma to his heart and left lung. At least two blows were delivered by a long thin blade. Maybe a switchblade, but I'm uncertain of that. His wounds reflect someone determined to ensure death. I don't think this was a street corner fight where the perpetrator would thrust once, then run away from the scene. This guy is probably practiced at knifing people because the killer's blade struck directly into the center of his victim's heart, then the left lung. Death came quickly. My full written report with all the details will be available by tomorrow morning. The DNA analysis will take a bit longer."

"The autopsy for Jason Beale is ongoing, but a preliminary report will be completed by the end of the day. But based solely on observation, he died of similar long puncture wounds to the abdomen and chest, resulting in massive hemorrhage."

Art pauses to take all this in. "Does it appear that the same or a similar weapon might have been used in the deaths of both men?"

"My sense is yes, but I need to determine that after completing the autopsy for Jason Beale."

Art thanks him for his work and the heads-up.

"Let's grab a bite to eat and clear our heads before knocking off for the day."

***

The next morning, Jack goes to work early, and checks in with the Office of Forensic Analysis to determine if latent prints were obtained from the glamour photos. John Riggs, who manages the office, informs him, "Unfortunately, the photos contain a series of smudges insufficient to characterize as fingerprints. We checked the front and backside of each photo."

Since the DNA blood specimen would be examined at the lab where John Riggs works, Jack expects a DNA profile to be produced from the unknown source of blood discovered on the body of Raymond. John confirms that a DNA profile was obtained for the unknown source.

"The problem, is that we don't know to whom it belongs. Once you acquire a probable suspect, we can do a comparative analysis, but until then, we're dead in the water. Do you have probable cause to get a DNA sample from a suspect?"

"Unfortunately, we don't.".

"By the way, Jack, we also ran the DNA through CODIS but didn't catch a match."

Art and Jack knock on Captain Grayson's door. She acknowledges their presence and invites them into her office.

Art takes the lead, "Captain, do you have a few minutes to speak with us?"

"Absolutely, indeed I do. Now, what good news do you have for me today, Lieutenant?"

"Well, you may not consider it good news, but I'll tell you about the latest developments with the Beale case."

"Okay, go ahead, I'm listening."

"Well, the latent fingerprint analysis for the glamour photos came back negative. So. we won't be able to determine a name until someone recognizes one of the photos and can identify him by name."

"Why is the photo ID so important, Lieutenant?"

"It's important because we're following your suggestion that we look into a gay lives angle that might be significantly linked to this case."

"Oh, okay now, I remember that, please continue."

"The Office of Forensic Analysis has developed a DNA profile on the unknown blood source taken from Julius Raymond's body."

"And why is this unknown blood specimen so important to this case, Lieutenant?"

"Because we believe the unknown DNA resulted from an inadvertent self-inflicted wound, by slippage or mishandling of the weapon used to kill Raymond. More importantly, we want to know why he was permanently silenced a day after Jack asked him to identify Beale's picture. As you'll recall, during our search of Beale's office, we also seized an appointment book containing the names of two men: Alan and Jeff. We believe there's a strong connection. Both name annotations with times were made within a couple of days of. Beale's death. Given that we've already interviewed Alan Jared, we plan to interview Jeff to assess his relationship to Mr. Beale and possible motive to kill him. We talked briefly with Jeff at his home but he wasn't very cooperative. We need to talk to him again."

CHAPTER ELEVEN

"Art, I have a crazy hunch."

"Okay, so what is it?" Your hunches have always been pretty accurate."

"Well, this guy Blanchard flew into a mini rage when we interviewed him. His behavior was inappropriate. Why would a man of his apparent wealth, influence, good looks, and business success fly off the handle over a series of non-accusatory questions? In my book, that makes him a suspect in our investigation."

"Well, we did ask him a couple of piercing questions that probably got under his skin. A lot of people may have reacted similarly. He may have thought we were attempting to somehow implicate him in the crime."

"Yes, but he was under no obligation to answer our questions, and he was probably aware of his rights. Look, the guy is big and tall, standing at least six-three, weighing in at about two hundred twenty pounds. He fits the height and complexion profile as described by the neighbor Pauline Clifton."

Art warns Jack, "We've got to tread lightly because we must avoid a citizen harassment complaint. The chief is very sensitive to such complaints. You know those are forwarded directly to his office for action and his direct response to citizens. Like his deceased partner, Kenneth Blanchard is probably on the mayor's list of generous reelection campaign donors. Given his behavior during the interview, let's get a background check just to know more about him."

"Okay, I'll make sure it gets done."

The next day, the background check for Kenneth Blanchard is complete.

Background Assessment

Name: Kenneth Blanchard

Address: Residence: 5944 Argonne Boulevard, New Orleans

Value of Home: $1,125,000

Vehicle: Mercedes Benz SL 500, valued at $167,000

Age: 37

Citizenship: American

Marital status: Single

Annual Income: $2,300,000

Telephone: 985-579-5848

Ethnicity: African American

Employment: Executive, co-owner FA&O Shipping LLC

Former Employer: NFL; New Orleans Saints Defensive End

Education: Bachelor of Science Degree, University of San Francisco, Human Relations and Organizational Behavior; Master's Degree, Tulane University, Business Administration

Military Service: None

Banking: Sutter Bank'erist

Hobbies: Knife throwing and collecting vintage knives

Habits/Vices: Expensive high end/imported cigars

Convictions: Charged with disorderly conduct for a bar fight

"Wow Art, this guy Blanchard looks squeaky clean except for an arrest for disorderly conduct, stemming from a bar fight. What stands out even more is his hobby. Apparently, he likes to tinker with knives!"

"I see that. Well, the bar fight speaks to me about his character. What we've seen of this guy on the exterior surface could be a false façade."

As the detectives are talking, the phone rings. Art answers and is surprised to hear the voice of Kenneth Blanchard.

"Good morning, Detective Beauregard. Look, Detective, I apologize for flying off the handle during our meeting. I guess I was just emotionally overwhelmed by the loss of my business partner. I knew that your questions were part of normal investigatory protocol, but feeling like I could possibly be a suspect was disturbing. Again, I apologize."

"Sir, apology accepted, but unnecessary. I appreciate your call, and thanks for reaching out to my partner and me."

Expressing a desire to be helpful, Blanchard offers to help, "If there is anything that I can do to assist you in furthering with your investigation, please let me know."

"Now that you mention it, I believe there is one other thing you might be able to help us with. Are you aware of the head-shot photos of men that were taken from Beale's desk as part of our search warrant?"

"Yes, I was briefed by my office of legal counsel."

"Good, then would you mind taking a look at the photos for possible identity?"

"Sure, I can do that, but you have my attention, and I'm curious," he says. "What seems to be the connection between the photos and Jason's death?"

"It's just a hunch, sir. Sometimes we detectives come up with the strangest thoughts and ideas that may not make sense, but we follow up to ensure a thorough and complete investigation, especially when we might be nearing the end of the investigation."

Art thinks to himself, *What a bunch of bullshit I just came up with while talking to a possible murder suspect!*

But it is sufficiently convincing because Blanchard acquiesces, "Okay, I can meet with you later this afternoon."

"We can quickly meet with you at your headquarters, or would you prefer to meet with us in one of our interview rooms? It shouldn't take more than a few minutes."

Later that afternoon, Blanchard is comfortably seated in an interview room at police headquarters. Art enters the room and asks Blanchard if he'd like a cup of coffee or water, since those are the only beverages available.

"Thanks for offering, Detective, but I'll pass."

Just as Art is about to speak, Jack enters the room holding the glamour photos. Jack greets Mr. Blanchard with an extended hand for a handshake. Jack mentally notes there are no apparent cuts or scrapes on his hand, but he can't see any skin above the wrist. Once the handshake is completed, Jack takes a seat and lays out the photos across the conference table.

"Have you ever seen any of these men?"

Blanchard reaches with his right hand to lift one of the pictures, then secures it in place with the fingers of his left hand. Jack then notices what appears to be a bandage on the fleshy inner portion of his right hand.

"Oh my goodness, what happened to your hand?"

"Oh, I cut myself while handling one of the knives in my collection. It's my hobby, collecting vintage knives from all over the world."

"Oh, I see."

Blanchard shakes his head. "I'm sorry, but I don't recognize either of these men."

"Thank you. We appreciate your taking valuable time out of your schedule to look at the photos."

As Blanchard leaves the interview room, the detectives offer their business cards and request that he call them if he can further help with their investigation.

After Blanchard is gone, Jack lets Art know he is not convinced by Blanchard's explanation. "I think it's more than coincidence that this guy has sustained a wound to his hand, near the time his business partner is slaughtered by force of a knife. We need a sample of his blood to compare it to the unknown contributor's blood found on the body of Julius Raymond."

"It's too bad he didn't accept our offer of a beverage because we could have tested it for DNA match," Art says. "The challenge here will be to find probable cause to demand a sample of blood, saliva, or tissue for DNA analysis and comparison. This is complicated by the fact that we don't have probable cause to demand anything at all from Mr. Blanchard." He shakes his head. "I feel like we've gotten nowhere."

A short while later, Captain Grayson steps from her office and shouts across the room, requesting Lieutenant Beauregard's presence in her office. "Please have a seat, Lieutenant." She immediately launches into the reason for his summons: "I just got a call from the chief. He told me that Blanchard called to discuss donating to his campaign for mayor. Coincidentally, he asked the chief why the department hasn't identified and arrested the men shown to him in a photo array by detectives working on the case. He further explained to the Chief that he believed those very same men may have been responsible for his partner's death. Further, Blanchard apparently told the chief that he didn't want to be bothered any more about the loss of his partner. The Chief assured him that he would look into it right away. I also learned today that Blanchard has given generously to the chief's campaign for mayor. Talk to me, Lieutenant."

Art blows out a huge sigh. "Captain, this is a clear attempt by Mr. Blanchard to undermine our investigation. His effort to place blame on the men in those photos is nothing more than a red herring. We have reason to believe that Blanchard himself could be responsible for the death of his partner, as well as Raymond, both of whom were viciously killed with the use of what we believe to be a long knife. The perpetrator was quite strong because Raymond was nearly decapitated by the force of a single slicing motion of the knife. It just so happens that our background check on Blanchard reveals that he is a collector of vintage knives, collected from all over the world. We noticed earlier today during his interview that he was wearing a bandage on his right hand. When asked about it, he told us he accidentally cut himself while handling a knife from his collection. We don't believe that for a second.

We also question his character based on a prior arrest for disorderly conduct, resulting from a bar fight. We want to compare his DNA to the unknown contributor's blood found on Raymond, but we don't have probable cause to compel Blanchard to submit to DNA comparative analysis. Now he's trying to influence our case through the chief's intervention. This is clearly intended to steer us away from viable suspects and take the investigation in another direction. If he's our man, he's a very shrewd and cunning customer. The worst kind."

"Okay," Madelyn interjects, "have you considered securing his DNA via surreptitious means?"

"We tried that already, but he refused an offer to drink a beverage while we interviewed him here in the building. So that didn't work. Any other surreptitious means of obtaining DNA would require your approval for additional money and police resources."

"Look, Lieutenant, during my conversation with the Chief, he said Blanchard was planning to attend some sort of class reunion event at his alma mater in San Francisco, sometime next week. Do you get my drift, Lieutenant?"

"Yes, I believe so, Captain, but do I have your approval for the additional money and resources needed for the operation?"

"Lieutenant, if this guy is as dangerous as you believe he is, we need to proceed with stealth and speed to get him off the street. I'd like for you to consider doing this: Develop a line-item cost estimate and put it on my desk by close of business today. I'll also need an outline of your plan to surreptitiously obtain Blanchard's DNA. You and your crew will be traveling. In order to maintain the highest degree of anonymity, Detective Sergeant Fratelli will not be part of the mission. I want to keep him back to continue the investigation locally."

As a result of her directives, Art and Jack set out to create the requested line-item cost estimate:

Cost Estimate:	Required Resources:
$3,600.00	3 days of pay for 3 plainclothes officers
$1,700.00	Roundtrip airline travel for 3 police officers
$3,100.00	Lodging and meals for 3 officers
$ 500.00	Incidentals
$8,450.00	*Total approximate cost*

Action Plan:

Mission Goals and Objectives: *Observe subject during all travel and at all times while away from the hotel where lodged. Surreptitiously obtain subject's DNA from items such as eating utensils, drinking containers, discarded tobacco products, discarded chewing gum, or any other source that might yield the subject's DNA. Ensure the police chain of custody for any and all possible DNA is maintained at all times in strict compliance with evidence protocol.*

Process:

Plainclothes officers (2) unknown to the subject will board the same airline flight to San Francisco and return flight(s).

Stake out the lobby of subject's hotel, observing subject's activity within confines of the building.

Follow and observe the subject at class reunion event, other events/places with the intent to surreptitiously obtain subject's DNA for analysis.

As necessary, use disguises to alter officers' appearance to avoid detection by the subject.

Undercover officers must maintain anonymity and appear as inconspicuous as possible.

Avoid direct contact with the subject and protect selves at all times.

Maintain standard buffer distance between officers and the subject.

Lieutenant Beauregard shall manage and monitor mission operations via regular text messaging and voice communications with officers assigned to this surveillance detail. He will also maintain a minimum out of sight distance between his team of officers, to avoid detection by the suspect.

Plainclothes officers selected for this surveillance mission to San Francisco are:

Detective Brian Broderick and
Detective David Stoddard

All officers are graduates of the FBI's Academy at Quantico, Virginia, where they were trained in advanced surveillance techniques and procedures. They are experts at what they do, and have over ten years of experience in the field.

***

It is late afternoon when Captain Grayson meets with Art to review the cost estimate and Action Plan for the mission to San Francisco.

"I'm approving this project as you've outlined because if true, this man is a menace and a serious threat to the citizenry of this community, and any other community. We must take all necessary action to protect the people from a dangerous psychopath. Although you'll be operating under the aegis of the New Orleans Police Department, San Francisco PD has been alerted to your presence and mission. Immediately upon your return from San Francisco, I'll expect a verbal briefing, accompanied by your written after-action report. Any questions Lieutenant?"

"No, Captain."

"Go forth, and please be very careful. This could be a very dangerous man."

Could this dangerous man be Kenneth Blanchard, a sophisticated, self-confident, and shrewd individual? Blanchard has a keen sense of awareness, and is very sensitive to people who are within his physical comfort zone—a sixth sense, almost. As he disembarks the plane after landing at San Francisco International Airport, he quickly glances to his rear, looking for anything out of place. He sees nothing that would alert him to the presence of an adversary of any kind.

However, as he glides along the escalator leading to the baggage claim area, his keen senses instinctively alert him to an unknown presence. Not knowing exactly what he has detected, he refuses to look to the rear, left, or right because he doesn't want to signal his awareness of what he believes might be a tail. He realizes that to be unnoticed, a tail will maintain a distance sufficient to view the subject from the longest feasible range. For that reason, a tail will normally not come within twenty feet of a subject.

Once Blanchard reaches the baggage claim area, he quickly surveils the area, searching for a standout who might be observing him. If his instincts are correct, he can only imagine why the New Orleans Police Department might have him under surveillance even when he is two thousand miles removed from that jurisdiction. He quickly spots a solitary man standing at a non-functioning baggage carousel with his head down, who seems focused on reading something held in his hand. Blanchard quickly makes a mental note of his clothing, approximate height, weight, and age. His facial features are obscured by dark sunglasses.

Once outside the terminal, Blanchard hails an Uber. Although he is apprehensive, the ride from the airport to his hotel is uneventful. It seems as if he is no longer being followed, so his concern for a tail has dissipated. Unbeknownst to him, two undercover detectives are following behind in a blue airport passenger van, hired solely for them. Art traveled to San Francisco a day earlier to become familiar with the hotel and the general area. He is in cell phone contact with his team of officers as they ride to the hotel.

While en route to his hotel, Blanchard opens his luggage and takes out a prized knife, the purpose of which is to admire its beauty, balance, and the sheer feel of power in his hand. He was careful to pack the knife within his checked suitcase to avoid detection. Because of a deep connection and near reverence Blanchard has for knives, he snugly places it in the breast pocket of his suit jacket for safe keeping.

Once the detectives arrive at the hotel, they hustle inside, where Detective Broderick reclines in a comfortable chair located at the far end of the lobby from which he can conduct surveillance. Blanchard reports to the front desk and routinely completes the registration process.

Blanchard once again is acutely aware of the presence of the mystery man from the airport. He knows that where there is one, there will be many, so he must remain calm while assuming there may be others who are interested in his activities in San Francisco. But he wonders why they are interested?

While Detective Broderick is closely watching the subject, Detective Stoddard decides to take a quick bathroom break, so he steps into a men's restroom adjacent to the main floor. Blanchard, who has decided to take a quick bathroom break after picking up his key, doesn't expect to see the man from the airport standing at the sink, washing his hands.

As soon as the two men make eye contact, Blanchard quickly recognizes the nearly imperceptible nervous twitch in Detective Stoddard's eyebrow. He also notices the bulge of a gun under Detective Stoddard's suit jacket. Blanchard looks away pretending not to notice Detective Stoddard whom he plans to kill.

Detective Stoddard, unsure if his cover has been compromised, quickly turns toward a toilet stall, when suddenly, Blanchard grabs his back the neck from behind. Stoddard desperately attempts to grab the handle of his service revolver, but Blanchard pulls his neck back and up, while with great speed and brutal strength, he produces one of his prized possessions made by an expert Japanese knife maker, which he uses to slash horizontally and deeply across Stoddard's neck. The brutality results in massive and immediate blood loss.

The struggle for life is intense and brief. Immediately, he releases Stoddard and allows him to tumble freely onto the cold floor of the men's restroom. Blood is everywhere. The assault takes all of ten seconds. With a sense of relief combined with nervous satisfaction, Blanchard quickly leaves the men's restroom. He doesn't normally conduct cowboy murders like this, but he's relieved there are no cameras in the area that could possibly link him to the approximate time that Stoddard also entered the men's restroom.

After ten minutes of unsuccessful attempts to reach Detective Stoddard via cell phone, Detective Broderick decides to conduct a physical search. Out of the corner of his eye, he observes a man running away from the area of the men's room, pointing back toward the area. The man's face is ashen and full of shock. Broderick can only think the worst. As he enters the men's room, he unintentionally steps into a large pool of blood. Immediately, he knows that Stoddard is beyond help, as his partner is nearly decapitated. The scene in the front lobby suddenly turns chaotic. An ambulance, police, and representatives from the coroner's office are dispatched and arrive at the hotel.

Any sense of completing his mission to tail Mr. Blanchard is overcome by Detective Stoddard's death, committed in such a brutal and brazen manner by a person unfit to exist among the living.

CHAPTER TWELVE

Inspector Clyde Millender of the San Francisco Police Department is alerted to the homicide of an out of jurisdiction police detective. Arriving at the scene of the crime, he assesses the body and the large pool of blood on the floor of the men's restroom. The presence of the body, combined with copious amounts of blood on the floor, is a horrible and gruesome scene.

Inspector Millender introduces himself to Detective Broderick, who tells the inspector who he is. "What happened here? We knew you were shadowing a man, but what the hell went wrong?"

"Detective Stoddard phoned to tell me he was going to take a leak. After ten or fifteen minutes, I tried to contact him, but he didn't answer. I started to worry, so I went to the men's room, and that's when I saw a guy who looked scared out of his mind running from the area of the restroom. I was hoping he wasn't running because something like this had happened. Once I entered the restroom, I could see immediately there was nothing I could do."

"Can you tell me about your mission here in San Francisco? Why were you here?"

"Well, we were conducting surveillance on our subject, but I'm pretty sure he was unaware of our presence."

"I'm aware of the surveillance. Your department informed me of it. Why were you tailing him, Detective?"

"It's because he was a strong suspect in at least one knifing homicide in New Orleans. It's possible that a second homicide could be attributed to our suspect."

"What is the suspect's name?"

"His name is Kenneth Blanchard. More specifically, Inspector, our mission was to secure DNA to match against a known foreign blood source left on the body one of our victims."

"I see. Detective Broderick, if we can help with gathering the DNA sample for analysis, trust me, you can rely on the San Francisco Police Department."

"Thanks, Inspector, appreciate it."

"Now, if there's nothing else, I need to talk to Blanchard. What's his room number?"

"He's in room 603."

"Thanks. Oh, by the way, Detective, find and hold the guy that ran away from the restroom because we need his statement. Have you contacted the New Orleans Police Department about this yet?"

"Yes, I called the Chief of Detectives, Captain Grayson. She's on her way to San Francisco."

Inspector Millender takes the elevator to the sixth floor and knocks on the door of room 603. After a long wait, the door is opened by Blanchard, who appears disheveled, as if just waking from sleep.

"Mr. Blanchard, good afternoon, I'm sorry to disturb you. I'm Inspector Millender with the San Francisco Police Department. Do you mind if I ask you some questions, sir?"

Mr. Blanchard frowns. "Why, what's going on, Inspector?"

"Well, there's been a knifing homicide in the hotel today and I was wondering if you may have heard or seen anything, sir?"

"No, Inspector, I haven't heard any noises or witnessed any unusual behavior. Who was the victim?"

"He was a police officer."

"Oh, I'm so sorry to hear that. Are you talking to everyone in the hotel?"

"As many people that may have heard or seen something, sir."

Blanchard gives the inspector a confused look. "Why would you think that I may have heard or seen something from here on the sixth floor?"

"Sir, that's because the murder occurred at about the same time you checked in, which is probably only a coincidence.

But we have to check everything."

"I wish I could help, Inspector."

"Okay, sir, please enjoy the rest of your day."

"Thanks, Inspector, I hope you find whoever did this."

Blanchard quietly closes his door and thinks about meeting old friends later in the evening at the class reunion event.

Captain Grayson arrives at San Francisco Police Headquarters and meets with Detective Broderick, Inspector Millender, and Art. She appears solemn and reserved, but Detective Broderick senses anger under her façade.

"The department has lost a good man. Whoever did this will suffer under the full weight and influence of the entire New Orleans Police Department. No one gets away with killing a cop. If our suspect is the perp, when he returns to New Orleans, we will eventually catch his ass." She gave a heavy sigh before continuing. "Inspector, is there anything that I can do or that you need from me to help catch the motherfucker that did this? And I don't apologize for my language. I'm so upset, I could chew leather."

"Well, I'll say this, Captain Grayson, I'm a bit suspicious about something that our suspect asked me."

"What was that, Inspector?"

"I thought it was strange when he asked me if anyone else was being interviewed, as if to send me in another direction, or conveying that he was insulted by my questions. He also gave himself an alibi when he mentioned that he couldn't have seen or heard anything from his room on the sixth floor. I thought that exchange was just a bit off-key, if you know what I mean. It was like a red herring. Why would he immediately offer reasons that might eliminate himself as a suspect?"

Not worrying about being a suspect, Blanchard eagerly prepares to attend the class reunion event this evening. Happy that the distraction of a nosy cop has been eliminated, he dresses in a beautiful navy-blue suit, produced by MarvelX Fashions. He strokes the sleeve of the suit coat as he admires it again, along with the beautiful matching red and blue silk tie. The suit clings to his muscular athletic frame, just as any expertly custom-made suit is expected to fit. He is especially pleased with the way his new ultra-soft leather loafers, produced by Bally, gently but firmly hug his size fourteen feet.

As he considers the possibilities for the evening, the table phone in his suite rings. "Hello.".

"Sir, the limousine you requested is parked and waiting for you at the front entrance."

"Thank you, I'll be right down."

The limousine driver warmly greets Mr. Blanchard while holding open the door. The interior of the vehicle is garnished with cigarettes, cigars, and a variety of warm and cold alcoholic beverages. A rack of magazines featuring a host of beautiful women with ample appeal and physical attributes is strategically placed for review.

Once underway, the driver confirms Blanchard's destination as the University of San Francisco. He also invites Blanchard to partake of the beverages and smoking options.

"Don't mind if I do." He unwraps a cigar, dragging it in front of his nose to inhale the richness of the aged scent. He lights the cigar and takes long drags, then exhales and smiles. As he enjoys the earthy aroma and smoothness of the cigar, he fans through one of several girly magazines, periodically raising his eyebrows as he proceeds through the magazine.

Two of San Francisco's finest have arrived at the class reunion before Blanchard. During the evening, the police personnel, disguised as a busboy and a waiter, keep an eye on the proceedings.

The evening is uneventful as Mr. Blanchard chats with various attendees. He appears to be in a good and festive mood. He has avoided foods offered this evening because of a personal obsession with maintaining his trim and muscular physique. Since his playing days as a member of the New Orleans Saints, his diet has consisted mainly of low-fat and cholesterol-free food items to help avoid weight gain. Notwithstanding his dietary restrictions, he is obsessed with body appearance and fitness, and he has only one health-threatening habit, which is his taste for high-end cigars.

At the end of the evening, Detective John Maxwell, who is in charge of the evening's surveillance team, calls Inspector Millender at home and informs him of the team's inability to collect a sample from Blanchard for DNA analysis. Disappointed, the inspector says, "Thanks, Detective, but we might have another option later."

Captain Grayson and Art return to New Orleans under deep sorrow and anger. She meets with Art and Jack to discuss progress on their caseload, saying, "I don't believe for a minute that the brutal use of a knife to kill Jason Beale, Julius Raymond, and Detective Stoddard were not intentionally committed by the same individual. The single thread that runs through each killing is Blanchard. He's fond of knives, he was a co-owner of his business with Mr. Beale and stood to gain financially from his death, and he was a guest at the hotel where Detective Stoddard was killed. Mr. Blanchard's connection to Mr. Raymond is unknown at this point in the investigation. Stoddard was brutally murdered, but we don't have an iota of evidence to name Blanchard as a suspect worthy of interrogation.

"So, Detectives, where do we go from here, and what about the Ivanov couple? Have you interviewed them again since the initial crime scene investigation?"

"No, Captain, Jack and I haven't, but it's on our to-do list for today, along with other case load requirements."

"We need to find out in a hurry where they are and why they disappeared so soon after Beale's death. It just doesn't make sense. Are they actually in hiding for some reason? What do they know about the murder of Jason Beale, if anything? Look, Detectives, this is the most pressing case within the department right now, and the chief is spitting bullets. He thinks that an unsolved murder involving a cop will not give voters great confidence in him when they show up at the polls to vote. Detectives, I want you dedicated exclusively to this case until solved.

With that in mind, I'm spreading out the balance of your caseload among other detectives. It's very expensive for a middle-aged couple to go into hiding, so they must have a source of funds not part of your background check. So, I suggest that you consider following the money. I want a daily verbal and written status report on your progress. Are there any questions, Detectives?"

"No, Captain."

Meanwhile, the luxury vessel carrying the special perishable cargo is scheduled to arrive at its destination, where a small fleet of trucks and men are waiting to unload and take charge of the cargo. The men hired will reload the cargo onto trucks for delivery along the eastern seaboard. The human cargo includes men and women, and their destinations are completely different. The women will be headed to the inner city of large metropolitan areas to work, while the men will be transported to farms and factories along the eastern seaboard to perform the type of labor many American men are reluctant to perform. Nadia Ivanov continues to maintain close and frequent contact with handlers on board the ship.

***

Miles away from the luxury vessel, unaware of the Ivanovs' nefarious activities, and frustrated that they are not closer to cracking the murder case, Art and Jack mull over their next plan of action. "Jack, following the money may not be the easiest thing to do because we don't know all the ins and outs of forensic financial analysis. So, who has the money in this case? Our choices seem to be potentially anyone that we've spoken to about the case. That would include the Ivanov couple, who seem to be in hiding; Katherine Parchisi, the lawyer; Julius Raymond, now deceased; and possibly Ms. Clifton, the neighbor. I think the path of least resistance where millions of dollars can be harbored and/or laundered, as necessary, resides within FA&O Shipping, given the three-million-dollar-plus value of Mr. Beale's home, and the million-dollar-plus value of the property owned by Raymond, who may be involved in all of that. And don't forget millions of dollars in income annually for Blanchard."

Art pauses to think for a moment before continuing. "I sense that this case involves nothing less than tens of millions of dollars. Controlling money is a classic struggle between the desire to spend money rather than hiding it."

"You're right about that Art, and the Captain is right when she suggested that we follow the money. Given that none of the valuables in the Beale mansion were disturbed or taken, I believe the killer is financially well off, so he has no reason to risk taking personal property and being caught with it in his possession. The only place remaining where large sums of money are controlled is with FA&O Shipping LLC. We could subpoena the company's financial records for audit."

Art counters that. "You know that won't wash because we don't have probable cause, and the company isn't suspected of cooking the books."

"Yeah, I get what you're saying Art, the obvious person with access to potentially millions of dollars might be Blanchard, but his financial background check is clean. Well, you would expect him to be clean because people who control illegally acquired monies don't usually invest in legitimate enterprises or financial institutions because the transactions result in audit trails. They are almost always hidden away in secret accounts within legitimate foreign financial institutions. We've got our work cut out for us."

As directed, Art and Jack meet daily with Captain Grayson to brief her on the status of the murder case. "Captain, Jack and I have worked the case for two weeks now, and frankly, we've hit roadblocks all along the way. As a result, our progress has been less than expected. It's not easy following the money, especially when we don't know who has millions of dollars in ill-gotten gains. I know that we must avenge the death of Detective Stoddard and solve the murder cases, but we don't know where to go from here."

"It sounds to me like you're making excuses, Lieutenant."

"No, Captain, I'm not making excuses. I'm saying we need help."

"There's got to be a better way to approach this thing." As she finishes her sentence, her phone rings. She frowns at the phone as though thinking about ignoring the call, but department policy requires all calls to be answered promptly, without exception. Reluctantly, she holds up a finger to Art and Jack and answers the call. As she listens to the person on the other end, she can hardly believe her ears or sit still. What she hears as she has her eyes focused on Art and Jack is a new and jaw-dropping development in the Saint Charles Avenue murder case.

The caller gives her the news in an enthusiastic tone. "Hello, Captain Grayson, this is Inspector Millender with the San Francisco Police Department. I hope you're doing well and sitting down."

Captain Grayson says, "Okay, so what's the bad news Inspector?"

"Well, I just received DNA analysis for a Mr. Kenneth Blanchard."

"How did you accomplish that, Lieutenant, while Blanchard is here in New Orleans?"

"Well, as you may recall, when Blanchard visited our fair city, he ordered a limousine to drive him from his hotel to a class reunion event at the University of San Francisco."

"Yes, he did, but I still don't understand your excitement."

"Well, it's simple, Captain. Lieutenant Beauregard of your department asked me to conspicuously place high-end cigars and other smoke products in the passenger compartment of the limousine, along with girly magazines, which we did. We managed to plant an undercover cop in the limo as the driver for the night. While en route to the University of San Francisco class reunion event, Blanchard accepted an offer to smoke tobacco products, which included high-end imported cigars."

Inspector Millender chuckled, proud that his intricate plan to trap Blanchard worked. "I guess it was irresistible because he took several puffs from the cigar. He doused the cigar in the ashtray. My undercover cop secured the cigar butt and submitted it for DNA analysis."

"Oh my god! How ingenious!" Captain Grayson exclaims. She pumps her fists and surprises the detectives as she does a slight shimmy. While briefing Art and Jack on her conversation, the three of them exchange several high fives, with smiles of triumph all around.

After being pumped up by the developments in the case, Art and Jack are ready to rumble the next morning, They and two uniformed police officers with a search warrant report show up unannounced at the headquarters of FA&O Shipping LLC. After instructing the security guard on duty not to notify anyone of their presence in the building, they board an unoccupied elevator and disembark on the seventh floor where the executive offices are located. Remembering the layout of the offices and conference room, the four men unceremoniously walk into Blanchard's suite of offices.

Blanchard quickly rises from his chair after observing and recognizing the detectives. He opens his mouth to speak but is quickly interrupted by Art. "Kenneth Blanchard, I have a warrant for your arrest for the murder of Mr. Jason Beale."

A collective, audible gasp is heard coming from employees attending a meeting in the executive conference room as a uniformed police officer approaches Blanchard, "Please turn around, sir."

Art is more than pleased to finally get to this moment after toiling over the case for weeks. "You're under arrest for the murder of Jason Beale. You have the right to remain silent. You have the right to an attorney, and if you don't have one, an attorney will be provided to you free of charge. Anything you say can and will be used against you in a court of law. Do you understand your rights?"

Blanchard invokes his right to silence. As the reading of his rights is completed, the uniformed officer places a firm grip around Blanchard's arm and escorts him to the elevator.

Frantically, Katherine Parchisi bolts into the suite. She identifies herself as legal counsel and says, "Lieutenant, what is going on here and why are you arresting him?"

With a stern face, Art calmly replies, "For Jason Beale's murder in the first degree, Ms. Parchisi."

Looking defeated, Blanchard says nothing as he is transported to central booking for fingerprinting and photos and assigned to a cell. He is arraigned the next day and pleads not guilty. Bail is set at $25,000,000.

CHAPTER THIRTEEN

Now that Blanchard has been identified as a suspect, solid evidence that he committed a crime needs to be collected. A warrant is granted to search Blanchard's residence. The focus of the search is to locate and identify any incriminating evidence that might be linked to the murder of Jason Beale, Julius Raymond, and/or Detective Stoddard. The seizure of a knife that might have been used in the commission of homicide could be tested for blood trace, and if found, tested and compared to the victim's DNA profile. The search of Blanchard's home results in seizure of twelve knives that were stored in a locked wall cabinet.

Given the brutality of the crime, District Attorney James Mason has announced his decision to personally prosecute the case. According to his deductions, the evidence for conviction far outweighs exoneration by a substantial margin. Given the overwhelming evidence against Blanchard, District Attorney Mason considers the circumstances to be a prima facie case. Securing a conviction is especially important if he expects to build on his reputation for success as a prosecutor. A conviction would send a firm message that he will not tolerate rampant crime. His skill and judgment as a prosecutor will be on full display for voters to assess. Winning could help catapult him into position as Mayor of New Orleans, or better yet, into the Governor's Mansion.

During the trial, District Attorney Mason plans on being steadfast in portraying Blanchard as an evil, vile person who has no regard for human life. He will argue that the jury not only convict Blanchard of triple murder in the first degree but that he should receive the death penalty as the most suitable punishment for such heinous crimes.

Both Mason and Chief of Police George Roberts are elated that a suspect has been apprehended in the brutal murder of Jason Beale. The Chief realizes that he must take immediate credit for solving the murders because his election as Mayor is at stake. Once again, this is his opportunity to demonstrate his oratory skills, while upgrading his profile as tough on crime. The more people he reaches with his tough on crime message, the better the chances he'll receive the most votes on election day.

District Attorney Mason coordinates with Chief Roberts to schedule a press conference to announce the arrest of Kenneth Blanchard. The Chief is once again flanked by Captain Grayson, Lieutenant Arthur Beauregard, and Detective Sergeant Jack Fratelli, but this time the district attorney, James Mason, is also present. All of them together in one place look like a "dream team."

Unlike when he spoke at the first press conference about the case, Chief Roberts is delighted to speak at this one. "Fourteen days ago, I reported the death of Mr. Jason Beale, who was a prominent member of our community. Today, I am pleased to announce the apprehension and arrest of a man suspected in the deaths of Mr. Jason Beale, Mr. Julius Raymond, and Detective David Stoddard. Seizing this opportune time to do a little campaigning, Roberts goes off script and does a little bit of self-promoting. I am totally committed to this case and am confident that under my supervision, my department will apply the full extent of our collective resources to bring justice in this case. Crime detection and prevention are my top priorities and I will work diligently to keep New Orleans safe, by being tough on crime, and compassionate to victims." Noticing that some people are looking at him quizzically, he abruptly stops his self-aggrandizing discourse, and gets back on script. "Yes, well, ah, the district attorney, Mr. James Mason, would like to impart a few words."

Mason steps to the mic, ready for his moment to shine. "Thanks, Chief Roberts. It's important that the community be made aware of the fact that the police department and the district attorney's office will not tolerate crime occurring within the greater metropolitan area of New Orleans. Perpetrators will be arrested and tried in a court of law. With regard to this matter, I've made the decision to personally manage and prosecute this case before the court. I have a proven track record as a tough prosecutor dedicated to upholding the laws of the criminal justice system. I promise I will use the full repertoire of my prosecutorial skills to convict this heinous villain and ask for the death penalty as a fitting punishment for three egregious and unforgivable crimes. "Are there any questions?"

"Mr. District Attorney, I'm Mike Flake with MCCS TV. What is the name and age of the person in custody for Mr. Beale's death and when do you expect he'll make bail?"

"The suspect's name is Kenneth Blanchard. The last name is spelled: B-l-a-n-c-h-a-r-d. He is thirty-seven years of age. Given his flight risk and financial means, my request to the court to hold him without bail was denied, but bail was set at twenty-five million dollars. I don't know if or when he'll make bail."

"Chief Roberts, I'm Paul Jagger with the Best News TV. Is Mr. Blanchard employed, and if so, where?"

"Mr. Blanchard is co-owner of FA&O Shipping LLC, which is based here in New Orleans."

"Chief Roberts, I'm David Craft with News Broadcast TV. Is Mr. Blanchard represented by counsel, and if so, by whom?"

"Yes, Mr. Blanchard is represented by his attorney, Ms. Katherine Parchisi."

"Would you please spell that last name, Chief Roberts?"

"Yes. It's P-a-r-c-h-i- s-i."

"Chief Roberts, I'm Cindy Blue, with the Evening Star TV News. Is there a known motive for commission of these crimes?"

"No, we haven't determined that, as yet, but we've got some leads and expect to uncover a motive by the time we go to trial."

"Chief Roberts, I'm Jeffrey Jules, with *Quick-News* magazine. Does Mr. Blanchard live within the city, and if so, what is his residential address?"

"Yes, Mr. Blanchard's address is 5944 Argonne Boulevard."

Sensing that enough information has been divulged, Ms. Debra Blackstone, director of the New Orleans Public Affairs Office, intervenes. "Ladies and gentlemen of the press, that concludes today's news conference. These officials have very busy schedules. Thank you."

The only official in attendance who is disappointed by Ms. Blackstone's announcement is Chief Roberts, who was thoroughly enjoying his exposure to the viewers and listeners, who are potential voters in support of his mayoral aspirations.

One person who was not focusing on the news conference was Katherine Parchisi. She was too busy scrambling to prepare a defense for her client. Although she is not considered one of the best lawyers in New Orleans, she is a passionate defender for her clients and goes out of her way to secure a favorable outcome for them. She knows that if she doesn't pull out all of the tricks of her trade, she will be booking a ticket straight to prison for Blanchard. She begins her trek for evidence by scheduling a telephone conference call with District Attorney Mason. As she waits for the conference call to populate with Mr. Mason and the assistant DA, Ms. Cross, she considers whether to argue or simply listen to the evidence against her client. She logically decides on the latter.

The district attorney enters the conference call where Katherine is patiently waiting for him. He is accompanied by the assistant district attorney, Michelle Cross. Once greetings and introductions are exchanged, they begin.

DA Mason is more than ready to get the conversation going. "Ms. Parchisi, you asked for this conference call, so how may I help you?"

"Well, Mr. District Attorney, I'm principally interested in the discovery of evidence accumulated against my client, Kenneth Blanchard. I would also like to know why he's being held under such an excessively high bail of twenty-five million dollars."

"Ms. Parchisi, under normal circumstances I would have met with you in person, but unfortunately, due to the logistics of my office, that was impractical. So please accept my apology."

"I understand, Mr. District Attorney. Thanks for conferencing with me."

"Ms. Parchisi, I'll be straight with you. We plan to secure a conviction, and subsequently, we will request that the court render a sentence of death for your client, Mr. Blanchard. We have a boatload of evidence, which includes DNA taken from a knife secured from your client's residence that matches all three victims—Jason Beale, Julius Raymond, and Detective David Stoddard. We also have unknown human DNA taken from other knives."

"Excuse me, that's implausible! Mr. District Attorney, are you serious? Do you have witnesses to the crime? Probably not. And what about the witness who claims to have seen an unknown man wearing a hat and long coat in the immediate area of the Saint Charles Street address where the crime was committed? Crime scene photos show voluminous blood at each site," Katherine is outraged. "Given the voluminous amount of blood at the scene of the crime, the perpetrator must have had blood splattered all over his clothing, so where are those items of clothing, Mr. District Attorney? That's missing evidence, sir, and could provoke reasonable doubt."

"Well, I guess we'll just have to see if a jury agrees with you, Ms. Parchisi, but I suggest that you speak candidly with your client about the mountain of evidence I'll be using at trial to convince the jury to convict and subsequently invoke the death sentence. No, we haven't yet uncovered the location of those outer garments. But we are attempting to determine if the DNA profile resulting from the swab of one of your client's knives matches any other recent assaults or deaths. I say again, the knives were all taken from your client's residence, as part of a vintage knife collection. Just something for you to consider.

"Ms. Parchisi, I'll also tell you this, DNA doesn't lie and we have lots of it linking your client to the brutal murders of our three victims. Moreover, we have a motive for the crime."

"And what would that be, sir?"

"Given the death of Mr. Beale, your client stood to become the sole owner of FA&O Shipping LLC. Your client would acquire Mr. Beale's thirty-percent ownership interest in the business, resulting in sole ownership, except for a smattering of smaller investors. Any way you cut it, that's motive; greed and financial gain. Please also know that one of our police officers was stabbed and killed while on duty in San Francisco. We don't take kindly to police officers killed in the line of duty. We found traces of his blood on one of the vintage knives taken from Mr. Blanchard's knife collection.

If that's not enough for you, Ms. Parchisi, we also have a DNA profile from a cigar that was smoked by your client.

That same DNA profile matches blood left at the scene of Julius Raymond's brutal murder."

Katherine is taken aback, the thought of defeat fleets through her consciousness. She shakes it off and regains her composure, determined to forge ahead and ignore the stop signs represented by what she has just heard. "This will be a very expensive and protracted trial, Mr. District Attorney."

"Are you suggesting already, Ms. Parchisi, that we enter into some kind of plea agreement?"

Katherine hides her frustration regarding all she has heard from DA Mason, and now speaks clearly and confidently. "Well, the burden of proof is with you, sir, but if you want to save money for expert witness testimony, and save the court's time, I'm willing to discuss it with my client, but my sense is he'll fight you all the way, and I will help him do that. Have a good day, Mr. Mason, and to you as well, Ms. Cross." The conference line closes.

CHAPTER FOURTEEN

Katherine has more at stake than losing this case, she will suffer a more personal loss if the one she loves is imprisoned. She is despondent that her lover, Kenneth Blanchard, has been incarcerated at the Orleans Parish Prison, charged with three counts of first-degree murder. She realizes that legally representing him may cloud her judgment and decision making. She visits the prison to speak with him and bring him up-to-date on what has happened with the investigation. Kenneth is tired and walks sluggishly into a small interview room, while a guard observes his every move just a short distance beyond the closed door.

"I am so glad to finally see you dear Katherine, I just want to hold you, but was told that we can't embrace."

"Yes, I know. They told me the same thing. Sweetie, do you need anything? You look worn out."

"Yes, I'm exhausted, I can't sleep, this place is noisy as hell. These crazy wackos are constantly yelling and screaming about how they were illegally arrested. It seems nobody is guilty of anything in here. That's the kind of constant insanity that comes out of the cellblock. The chief security officer, Randy Wade, is an old college classmate from USF. He's tried to make me as comfortable as feasible. He's always been a loyal friend."

"That's encouraging, I'm glad your friend is here for you, sweetie. I'm desperate to get you out of here soon, but for now, let's talk about your case. The evidence the district attorney claims to have against you seems overwhelming in support of a conviction if we go to trial. Once I receive their evidence, under discovery, I'll be able to assess the true strengths and weaknesses of the DA's case. Simultaneously, I'll try to schedule a bail reduction hearing so you can come home while your case is pending.

"When I met with DA Mason and the assistant DA earlier today, he claims they have a cigar butt that you smoked on the way to the class reunion event. The resulting DNA profile could be used to match you to blood found on the body of Julius Raymond. Another claim is having a DNA profile from one of the vintage knives seized at your home that matches Detective David Stoddard's DNA profile. Also, they are supposed to have to have a DNA profile from one of the knives in your vintage collection that matches Jason Beale's DNA profile. Given the weight of those claims, collectively, I informed the DA that I would candidly discuss with you the state of the case.

"Mason was blunt today when he informed me that conviction, in this case, will result in arguing for and requesting the death penalty." At the mention of those two words, "death penalty," Katherine breaks down into tears. The thought of the death penalty handed down for Kenneth is hard to fathom.

Ignoring her tears, Kenneth focuses on getting himself proven innocence. "So, Katherine, what kind of defense are you considering for me?"

"Before we discuss that, there's one other thing you need to know about that was discussed with the district attorney. I floated a proposal that you cop to a plea for a lesser charge. Surprisingly, the DA seemed somewhat receptive to the possibility, but he may have been disingenuous. They'll lie and do almost anything to win cases as part of a concerted effort to improve their political standing within the community. I further suggested that the City would probably save money for expert witness testimony while saving the court's time."

Kenneth's delighted to hear of an option that may make him a free man. "And that would save me from the death penalty, right?"

"I would have to negotiate that point, but yes, it might work. Please understand, sweetheart, that law enforcement personnel are very sensitive to cases of homicide involving a police officer while serving in the line of duty. Listen, take some time to think about how you'd like to proceed with the case, but in the meantime, I'll share with you my opinion on how best to proceed. I'll also be working on reducing your bail so you can come home to me." After a long pause, and with more tears in her eyes,

Katherine reluctantly ends the visit, "Bye, sweetie, I'll see you tomorrow."

Fueled by being overjoyed to see Kenneth, Katherine dives into completing the tasks necessary to free her lover. She starts with scheduling a hearing for Kenneth's bail reduction. The judge in the case, Carlton Clinton, is considered friendly because rumor has it he is not fond of the US bail system because he believes it is unfair to many indigent crime suspects. Individuals who are more likely to be held in jail in lieu of bail are the poor and less-well-to-do people. Affluent citizens are usually able to make bail and be released from confinement.

In Judge Clinton's opinion, the bail system is an archaic and unequal process that provides the path of least resistance for individuals who are sufficiently funded to be released from jail, pending trial. As a result of rumors floating around the court, Katherine's maneuvering has resulted in the hearing being assigned to Judge Clinton and scheduled for this Thursday.

***

At 9:00 a. m. on a cloudy, breezy Thursday, the bail reduction hearing gets underway when the court clerk announces, "The court will now come to order. Judge Carlton Clinton presiding."

"Today we're here to consider a request to reduce bail in case number 579584. Present is Michelle Cross representing the District Attorney's Office. Is the plaintiff present, and represented by counsel?"

"Yes, your honor, Kenneth Blanchard is present and represented by counsel Katherine Parchisi."

"I understand this hearing is being held to determine if the bail amount should be reduced. Current bail is set at twenty-five million dollars. I'll now hear from Ms. Parchisi."

"Your honor, bail is excessive. My client is a well-respected member of the community. He has deep business and personal roots therein as a homeowner, business owner, and employer of hundreds of people. He does not represent a flight risk, and the success of his large business enterprise depends on his presence to manage. My client is receptive to wearing an electronic tracking device, if necessary, your honor. Thank you, your honor, for considering bail reduction."

"Thank you, Ms. Parchisi. "Ms. Cross, I'll now hear from the district attorney."

"Thank you, your honor. The government will prove in pending trial that Mr. Blanchard killed three people from within our community, one of whom was a police detective assigned to the New Orleans Police Department. As a result, Mr. Blanchard is a danger to the community and society in general. Given the seriousness of his crimes and financial means, he is a flight risk. We respectfully request that bail reduction be denied. The District Attorney's Office believes bail set at twenty-five million dollars is appropriate."

"Thank you. I'm ready to make my decision. Bail is generally set based on four important factors of consideration, the seriousness of the event or crime, the criminal history of the accused, which in this case is nonexistent, the probability that the accused will flee the jurisdiction of the court, and whether public safety might be placed in jeopardy. Accordingly, I've considered all of this, and find that the current court-ordered bail is appropriate. In light of that, a request for bail reduction is denied."

Ms. Cross smiles, satisfied that Blanchard, who she thinks is a menace to society, will not be able to post bail and be on the streets again. "Thank you, your honor."

***

In contrast, Parchisi is infuriated and abruptly storms out of the courtroom and makes a bee line to the Prison. Still feeling remorse about not being able to secure bail reduction for Kenneth, Katherine solemnly enters the gates of the Prison to give Kenneth Blanchard the negative outcome of the hearing. She waits in a small room surrounded by glass for Kenneth to appear. Once again, he is exhausted and feeling oppressed, except now he is badly in need of a shave. He looks awful, she thinks to herself.

Once she's seated at the table opposite Kenneth, and the door is closed, she looks into his blood-shot eyes. "Sweetie, I tried to reduce bail but clearly the district attorney wants you held as some form of punishment. His strategy is obvious—he wants something from you. Whatever it is, if you provide it, he can take the death penalty off the table."

Kenneth is furious about the decision, but he has devised a plan to get out of jail. "Do you have any idea what he might want to talk about?"

"No, but I can ask him to visit us here at the prison to discuss your case if that's what you'd like me to do. We just need to feel him out to see what he wants, if anything."

"Look, sweetie, here's the plan, I want you out of this mess because I anticipate that it's going to get nasty. I don't want to jeopardize your career or safety, so this is what I need you to do. I've thought hard about this, so please don't dismiss it offhand. I want you to visit the local Actors Guild, the purpose of which will be to contract with an actress to play the role of your double. Now listen carefully. In order to fund the plan that I have in mind, please withdraw from my special location, one point one million dollars."

Katherine starts out early the next day, anxious to set Kenneth's plan in motion. She checks in with the local Actors Guild. After reviewing multiple portfolios and speaking with staff members and potential acting candidates, Katherine interviews a young woman named Consuela, who surprisingly could be her double in real life. Consuela has clearly demonstrated her ability to play the role of an attorney, as Katherine describes it. Katherine further explains that she will perform her role in disguise. She also informs Consuela that the role she'll play could possibly require several meetings with two politically powerful men. She tells her that the job pays $10,000, with half paid in advance and the rest paid a couple of days after she completes her acting role.

Katherine hands Consuela an envelope containing $5,000 in cash. The woman is ecstatic about the offer, and accepts the initial cash payment, then listens carefully as Katherine details her character and performance. "One last thing, Consuela. You cannot tell anyone about this job, ever, not even your children. Do you understand, promise, and agree?"

Consuela quickly agrees, letting nothing get in the way of earning the much-needed cash. "Yes, I really need the

money. I have two small children, and I'm a single parent."
She tightly clutches the initial $5,000 as if it might fly away.

Katherine gives the woman an incentive to remain silent, "If you've remained silent after one year, you'll be given a bonus payment of an additional ten thousand dollars. Should you ever speak to anyone about this acting job, the bonus will not be paid. Is this all very clear?"

"Absolutely! Yes, yes, I understand."

"Finally, I will contact you daily to provide instructions."

"Okay, but will I get into some kind of trouble for my role?"

"I guarantee that your role will not require that you perform an illegal act. Your last name for this role is Parchisi. It's spelled P-a-r-c-h-i-s-i. Is that clear?"

"Yes, it's very clear, I will remember it."

The phone rings on the district attorney's desk. "Hello, this is District Attorney James Mason."

"Mr. Mason, this is Katherine Parchisi, calling on behalf of my client, Kenneth Blanchard."

"Oh yes, your client, but isn't he more than that to you, Ms. Parchisi?"

Failing to respond to his insulting witticism, Katherine stays professional. "My client would like to speak with you concerning an important matter."

"Excuse me, Ms. Parchisi, but that would be highly irregular, and possibly unethical. For what purpose would I want to speak with your client? I already have a prima facie case against him, and I will easily prevail."

"Sir, that is your opinion and decision. My client isn't exactly begging you to discuss actions that might further assist you in your obvious effort to ascend to the governor's office."

There is a pause before DA Mason replies, "Very interesting, Ms. Parchisi. I can meet at the prison with you and your client tomorrow at eleven a.m. sharp."

Once seated at the prison in the small conference room with Katherine and Kenneth, DA Mason begins his query. "So, is there something you need from me, Mr. Blanchard?"

"Yes, there is. I want you to take the death penalty off the table."

Katherine is taken aback by his statement, but her antennae are in high-alert listening mode.

DA Mason looks amused as he sits back in his chair. "Now why would I do that, Mr. Blanchard?"

"Because you'd be deemed a hero by the media. You could indict me and my accomplices for engaging in large-scale criminal operations. In exchange for my self-incriminating confession, accompanied by revelations of large-scale illegal criminal operations, my bail must be reduced sufficiently to allow me to be released from jail, pending trial." Kenneth thinks to himself that he has given Mr. District Attorney sufficient incentive to make it all happen. Kenneth, however, has an intricate plan that runs counter to the story he has just imparted.

"Well, sir, I can say that you have my complete and undivided attention. What specifically would you like to confess?"

Kenneth shakes his head as Katherine remains silent. "Not so fast, Mr. District Attorney. I want our agreement in writing and signed not only by you, but by the chief of police, George Roberts."

"That might be insurmountable, Mr. Blanchard."

"It's required in order to reach the governor's office, Mr. Mason."

"Mr. Blanchard, how would you propose that I influence and convince the chief of police to sign a document that's unethical as hell, and probably borderline illegal?"

"That's quite simple, actually. All men have unsatisfied needs and desires, so help him ascend to the position he has salivated over for many years."

James Mason narrows his eyes. "And what might that be, Mr. Blanchard?"

Well, it's the office of Mayor, of course. As governor, you could make that happen through financial endorsement, radio announcements, TV ads, the influence of your vaunted office, and highlighting his many skills and experiences as chief of police that have prepared him to hold political office.

"Our written agreement must be ironclad, and written by someone highly skilled in the business of drafting sensitive agreements—non-disclosure agreements, airtight prenuptial agreements and the like."

Katherine is a bit dumbfounded as she sits listening to this scheme, as discussed by a criminal and a law enforcement official. She's quite nervous because she's now complicit as a party to this apparent scheme of insanity.

Kenneth continues to explain what must be done. "Mr. Mason, this is a caveat: Our written agreement must be executed within the next three days, and each of us will receive an original of the executed document. Agreed?"

"I need to think about this"

"That's fine, but time is of the essence, you should not allow the opportunity to achieve your dream to simply fade away."

Later that day, while reflecting on his conversation with Blanchard, the district attorney considers the implications of acting affirmatively regarding Blanchard's scheme. If he buys into it, the first challenge will be getting the Chief of Police, George Roberts, to endorse the binding contract agreement. The second challenge, although less daunting, will be to have Blanchard's bail sufficiently reduced to provide him the freedom to pursue his livelihood and way of life, at least temporarily. The third challenge will be to draft the binding agreement, producing three original copies that will be signed concurrently by the three parties.

CHAPTER FIFTEEN

Acting to solve his dilemma, and attempting to fulfill his role in the scheme, District Attorney Mason picks up the phone on his office desk and dials the phone number to the office of Chief of Police George Roberts. The phone rings, and he's immediately transferred to George Roberts.

"Hello, this is Chief Roberts."

"Chief Roberts, this is District Attorney James Mason."

"Great to hear your voice, Mr. District Attorney. What's on your mind today?"

"Well, Chief, I just want to congratulate you on the way you managed the news conference the other day. You were in fine form while conveying strength and confidence to the voters of our great city."

"Well, thank you, Mr. District Attorney, for your cogent and inspiring comment. I appreciate that greatly."

"Chief, have you ever considered running for higher political office?"

"I'd be disingenuous if I said I never had such thoughts and aspirations, sir," the chief admits, smiling broadly.

"Chief, I'll get straight to the point. There are high echelon business leaders and other prominent authorities operating in the deep shadows who tend to canvass the community for highly qualified men and women who can lead the way in politics and law enforcement. I think there may be a path forward for you to pursue such an initiative, but secrecy is absolutely essential. Would you be interested in meeting with me, and possibly others, at a private location to discuss how this might happen for you? Before you respond, Chief, let me say that this initiative is not for the squeamish."

"I understand completely. Where would our meeting take place?"

"Are you available at seven p.m. this evening?"

"Yes, I can be available."

"Wonderful. Your police uniform would stick out like a sore thumb, so in order to lower your profile, please wear a business suit. The meeting location is the JW Mercury Hotel, located in the French Quarter. If this all sounds too mysterious, please tell me now, whereas I can inform other leaders that you're undecided."

"No, no, I'm committed and will meet with you this evening at seven p.m., Mr. District Attorney."

"Happy to hear it. Please check in at the front desk, and ask for a note left in your name. Thanks, Chief, and please don't be late."

Chief George Roberts reports to the front desk of the JW Mercury Hotel and retrieves a note from the front desk clerk. As he stands there, he reads the note: "Please use the house phone on the left side of the lobby to call room 1206." He dials the number, and a male voice answers and requests that he report to room 1101.

Unknowingly, George Roberts is being surreptitiously watched to ensure he's not being followed and doesn't use his cell phone. Nothing appears suspicious about his movements or behavior, and he does not appear to have been followed.

Once he arrives at room 1101 and believes that he has not been noticed, he knocks on the door, it's opened by District Attorney James Mason.

"Thanks for coming, Chief, and for being on time. May I offer you a beverage before we get underway? We have soft drinks, as well as alcohol. What would you like?"

"I would enjoy a taste of Hibiki Whisky, neat if you have some."

"Chief, we just happen to have it over here on the bar, although it's rare to find it available. Please serve yourself.

I apologize for all of the cloak and dagger, but we must be certain of secret communications. Please have a seat, Chief. This evening, I'll be the only principle involved in our meeting. Oh, by the way, can we dispense with our titles? I'd prefer that you call me James."

"And likewise," says the chief, "please refer to me as George."

"This, you agree, would only apply in private settings, such as this." When Chief Roberts nodded, Mason got down to business. "Great, now let's talk about the reason I'm here. Your ascension to the position of mayor of this city is nearly assured, accompanied by the financial wherewithal and political will behind your candidacy. There are strings attached, however."

"Strings, what kind of strings?"

"Yes, it involves a bail reduction for one of the city's high-profile and prominent citizens. He's currently being held at Orleans Parish Prison on a homicide charge. The case against him is prima facie, and I plan to personally lead the prosecution of the case.

"Reduction of his bail will allow him to manage his very large business enterprise, employing hundreds of people, pending trial, of course. I believe I can manage to get his bail reduced, after some initial resistance from the court. My responsibility, along with yours, would require that we sign a binding agreement, in support of Kenneth Blanchard."

"Do you have the agreement now? Can I can read it?"

"It's being drafted right now and will be ready sometime tomorrow for review and signature. These types of things are often done in support of worthy causes by my group of concerned businessmen. Can we count on your support and participation?"

"Yes, but subject to review of the binding agreement."

DA Mason nods affirmatively. "Okay, George, fair enough. And again, George, this is a matter to be held in the strictest of secrecy. If anyone were to ever ask me about this or any other meeting that we might have now or while you're serving as mayor, I would categorically deny it."

The chief judge for the municipal court is the Honorable Hiram Pitts, who has sat on the bench in excess of twenty-five years. During his tenure, he's seen matters ranging from the sublime to the ridiculous. This day, he receives an unusual call from District Attorney James

Mason, whom he has known personally for a decade or more.

"Great hearing from you James, how have you been? I haven't seen you since last year's Christmas party."

"I'm feeling great, Hiram, except for a few aches and pains in my joints."

"Hah! I can certainly identify with that."

"Hiram, I have a dilemma that I need to unravel, with your assistance, if possible. Recently, there was a hearing to reduce bail for a prominent businessman charged with homicide. My assistant attended the hearing on my behalf. Unfortunately, she argued against bail reduction. The defendant is an upstanding member of the community who owns valuable property in the community and the owner of a large business in which he employs hundreds of our citizens. He's certainly not a flight risk. Although I feel that his pending trial presents a prima facie case, I've heard his plea to allow him out of custody with the freedom to manage his company and other personal affairs. He has expressed a willingness to wear an electronic monitoring device. Is there any way that you can intervene and assist in this matter?"

"Without any guarantee, I'll look into it and get back to you."

"Thanks, Hiram."

It's crunch time, and Katherine has a million things to do to ensure that her and Kenneth's scheme works. On behalf of Kenneth, she , Katherine Parchisi makes a call to the district attorney.

"Hello, this is the Office of the District Attorney. How may I direct your call?"

"This is attorney Katherine Parchisi. Is Mr. Mason available to speak with me?"

"Please hold." A few minutes later the woman comes back on the line. "Ms. Parchisi, the district attorney has asked that you contact the assistant DA, Ms. Cross. Do you have her number, ma'am?"

Katherine, a bit befuddled, sputters out with a wave of her hand, "No, no, that's okay. Thanks."

Immediately after hanging up, her phone rang, showing an unknown caller and telephone number. The district attorney is on the other end of the line. "Ms. Parchisi, from this point forward, please do not call my office phone. What is the nature of your call?"

"It's about the binding contract agreement. My client has instructions for drafting the document. There's also a trust issue that must be worked through so all parties are comfortable and confident with the contract.

My client proposes a requirement that the three of you meet with me to receive his confession and concurrently sign the binding agreement. In the final analysis, the document is signed by the three of you. This would require his release from custody to bring this to fruition."

"By three, you mean Chief Roberts, me, and your client slash boyfriend?"

"Mr. District Attorney, I don't take kindly to insults from bullies. Please apologize, or I'll inform my client that you're not of the mind and temperament to proceed with the agreement.

The DA sighs, not really regretting anything he has said. "I apologize, please forgive me, Ms. Parchisi."

"Mr. District Attorney, my client has asked me to meet with you privately to discuss an important financial matter. Are you available?"

"Can you tell me more about the nature of the meeting, other than it's financial?"

"I'm not permitted to discuss this matter with you unless we're in a private and secure location. But please know that my client is impatient and time is of the essence."

"Does your client have a place in mind where we should meet?"

"Yes, but I will need to meet with you and Chief Roberts in one hour at 5944 Argonne Boulevard. Please arrive promptly, one hour from now. A considerable amount of money is at stake, so please be on time. I suggest you bring two large briefcases with you."

George Roberts, James Mason, and Ms. Parchisi (or rather, the actress playing Ms. Parchisi) meet at Kenneth Blanchard's house and sit down to talk. The actress, Consuela, as enacted a clever way to partially disguise herself to avoid recognition as an imposter. She tells everyone she is embarrassed by the scarf covering a part of her face due to a nasty case of psoriasis that she's being treated for by her doctor. "Gentlemen, please know that the property has been swept for electronic listening devices, and there are none." She goes on to explain that she is simply the messenger and that either man is free to leave, at will.

"Gentlemen, my client has tasked me to ask each of you several very important financial questions, the answers to which I will convey to my client, forthwith.

"Question 1: What would be your reaction this very evening if each of you were endowed with an immediate gift of five hundred thousand dollars in cash, tax-free?

"Question 2: What would be your reaction this very evening If each of you were given access to a million dollars in cash, every year for six years?

"Question 3: For six million dollars each, would you arrange to ensure that my client will receive a sentence of no more than five years, served at a club fed type of minimal security facility if found guilty in the murder of three people?

"Gentlemen, those questions were designed to evoke thought. I will hear from you now, but before you respond, let me tell you that over the next two years each of you could earn up to twelve million five hundred thousand dollars, tax-free. There is no scheme contrived here today. The intent of this meeting is to secure your commitment, after reviewing and signing the binding contract agreement. Each of you must sign the contract for it to be considered fully executed. Signing the document could make each of you rich beyond your dreams.

"Are you ready and willing to read the agreement?" When both men nod, she continues, confident that the scheme is working so far, "Given that my client is indisposed at this time, earlier today, he took the initiative to sign the document. It's now ready for your signatures."

Consuela removes two binding contract agreements from her valise and hands one to each man. As she observes the men reading the document, George Roberts looks at her occasionally with a frown. She says nothing. As the men continue reading, she observes James Mason raise an eyebrow. She thinks to herself that it might be a good sign. Then the two men look at one another and smile.

DA Mason says to Chief Roberts, "Maybe we should sleep on it overnight."

Immediately, Consuela interjects: "Gentlemen, the sunset for this important matter is this very evening. If the document isn't fully executed today, the contract opportunity ceases to exist."

DA Mason says, "How can we trust you and your client, Ms. Parchisi?"

"There's an old adage that goes something like this: The proof is in the pudding. My client is prepared to have you taste the pudding this evening," at which time she opens a large luggage carrier. She unzips the carrier and opens it to reveal two large bundles of money. "The one million dollars before you is to be divided evenly between the two of you."

The eyes of each man are suddenly fixed on the enticing million dollars in cash.

"As proof of good faith and as an incentive for your cooperation, the money is yours, but only after you sign the agreement."

The allure of the cash is irresistible, and convinces the men of the legitimacy of the contract, as bolstered by good faith money. The document is quickly signed by District Attorney James Mason and Chief of Police George Roberts. Their normally good judgment is obscured by greed and blind ambition. They are so excited and focused on counting and packing the money in their suitcases that they are now oblivious to the binding contract agreement bearing their signatures. The agreement, along with Mr. Blanchard's confession, reads as follows:

Binding Contract Agreement

This *Binding Agreement is between the parties hereinafter known as District Attorney James Mason; Chief of Police George Roberts; and Mr. Kenneth Blanchard, each of whom willingly and knowingly endorses and approves of this Binding Contract Agreement. This is further affirmed by the signatures inscribed at the end of this Agreement.*

First: I, Kenneth Blanchard, do hereby confess to the murder of Police Detective <u>David Stoddard</u>, wherein the city of San Francisco, I fatally stabbed him in the chest using a knife taken from my residence and vintage knife collection, under the authority of a valid search warrant.

Second: Further, I hereby confess to the murder of a citizen known as <u>Julius Raymond</u>, wherein the city of New Orleans French Quarter, I fatally stabbed him in the chest and sliced open his throat, using a knife taken from my residence under the authority of a valid search warrant.

Third: Further, I hereby confess to the murder of Mr. <u>Jason Beale</u>, wherein the city of New Orleans, Garden District, I fatally stabbed Mr. Beale in his chest and abdomen, using a vintage knife stored at my residence. The subject knife was taken from my home under the authority of a valid search warrant and is now in the possession of the New Orleans Police Department.

Fourth: In the case of Mr. Jason Beale and Mr. Julius Raymond, they both knew too much about matters related to my illegal business of smuggling human beings from overseas locations, who were hidden within large commercial ships that under normal operations would transport a wide range of commercial cargo. Over the course of the previous 5-year period, such illegal business operations have netted untaxed dollars on the order and magnitude of $25,000,000 annually.

Fifth: A $125,000,000 personal account, funded by my illegal smuggling operations, has been established with the Banco De Cayman Islands, under the fictitious name of George Marathon Runner, Account Number B46 095 331 A9KJ. As part of this Binding Contract Agreement, arrangements have been made to allow District Attorney James Mason and Chief of Police George Roberts to equally withdraw from said account no more than $500,000 each month, for up to 24 months.

The account is strictly monitored for activity by certain individuals, unknown to either of you. Such individuals are employed by Kenneth Blanchard and are paid handsomely each month from a separate account to ensure that I am released from prison, as stipulated herein. District Attorney James Mason and Chief of Police George Roberts have previously received good faith cash payments of $500,000 each, that were funded from my illegal smuggling activities.

Page 2 of 3

Failure to carry out the terms and requirements, as specifically outlined herein, will result in the closure of such account, followed by a vigorous search of the globe by unknown persons to locate and terminate District Attorney Mason and Chief of Police George Roberts.

Chief of Police George Roberts and District Attorney James Mason have collaborated and conspired with me to ensure the necessary actions are taken to exonerate me in pending trial or trials, and that, if I'm found guilty, I will serve no more than 5 years of incarceration in a minimal security facility, often referred to as Club Fed.

Joint failure of Chief of Police George Roberts and District Attorney James Mason to strictly and fully comply with the terms and conditions of this Agreement, as outlined herein, will result in unintended consequences, affecting themselves, and their respective families.

James Mason:_____   Date:_____

George Roberts:_____   Date:_____

Kenneth Blanchard:_____   Date:_____

----------------------*NOTHING FOLLOWS*----------------

Now that the binding contract and the deals have been agreed to, all parties involved must now fulfill their tasks. Although flush with illegal money, the district attorney and chief of police nonetheless focus on arresting everyone involved in the smuggling operation. They are also concerned about the impact that such arrests will have on their political careers and family life. Before considering the arrests, however, they have to concern themselves with reducing Blanchard's bail, resulting in his release from Orleans Prison.

District Attorney James Mason is reluctant to call Judge Pitts again, so soon after discussing the bail issue involving Blanchard. He knows that he has to lie low on the matter in order to avoid arousing any suspicion.

The next day, late in the afternoon, the district attorney receives an e-mail from an anonymous source. The message reads: "Why is my client still in jail?"

James Mason immediately deletes the e-mail. He senses that the anonymous message is from Katherine Parchisi. He whispers to himself, "That little bitch, doesn't she know it was only yesterday that we agreed to take the necessary action to help reduce bail for her killer boyfriend?"

Similarly, Chief Roberts receives the same e-mail. He is flustered and nervous but knows it is too risky to contact James Mason, so he advises his staff that he is leaving for the day to rest while his headache resolves.

Judge Hiram Pitts, the chief judge, picks up the receiver of his desktop phone and dials a phone number. Soon, the phone is answered by Judge Carlton Clinton. Judge Pitts greets him with a broad smile on his face, "Good morning, Carlton."

"Yes, good morning, Hiram, what's on your mind so early in the day?"

"Well, I want to discuss the bail hearing conducted a couple of days ago for Mr. Kenneth Blanchard. You presided over the hearing and denied the defendant's request for bail reduction."

"Oh, yes, I recall the case because the bail was quite high; twenty-five million dollars, if my memory serves me correctly. I believe he was charged as a suspect in a triple homicide."

"Well, the district attorney spoke with me about an excessively high bail in the case. He believes the assistant DA argued so strenuously to deny bail reduction that you ruled in her favor, to maintain the bail amount."

"Hiram, again, based on memory, I thought the argument offered by the assistant DA was plain and straightforward, without a strong pleading. She had the upper hand going in because the defendant was sitting on a possible death sentence for triple homicide. Releasing someone on that charge could potentially expose the community to significant risk. As a result, I let the bail stand. With respect to defense counsel, her argument was vanilla and gave no compelling reasons that would sway me into buying her argument for bail reduction. She simply failed to move the needle on emotion or strong justification for bail reduction. It was definitely not a strong argument."

"But Carlton, that doesn't line up with James Mason's effort to allow bail reduction. It just doesn't make sense. Carlton, it's known around the court that you have a disdain for the bail system in the country because it's unfair in the manner because people with money and means are treated differently than the poor and indigent, yet you maintained bail amount.

"Hiram, it was instinct and a gut reaction."

"Okay, Carlton, thanks for speaking with me."

Belinda Brock, the administrative assistant to Judge Hiram Pitts makes a call for him. The call is answered by District Attorney James Mason. "Hello, this is James Mason, how may I help you?"

"Mr. District Attorney, good afternoon, this is Belinda Brock, assistant to Chief Judge Hiram Pitts. He has a very busy calendar today, so he asked me to call and inform you that Mr. Kenneth Blanchard's request for bail reduction will continue at the current level. He also asked me to tell you that his phone line is always open to speaking with him."

The bad news hits James Mason like a flat brick upside his head. He immediately realizes Judge Pitts' decision could significantly impact his life and that of his family. He's flabbergasted to the extent that he catapults from his chair and walks over to the leather couch situated in a far corner of his office. He reclines on the couch to plan his counterreaction.

At 12:30 p.m., while the district attorney sits at his desk eating a meatloaf sandwich prepared by his wife, he hears an audible and familiar sound emanating from his desktop computer.

In response, he hits a couple of keys on the keyboard to reveal the e-mail message. It reads: "Since Kenneth Blanchard is still in prison, a meeting will be held today at the Argonne Avenue address. Be there at 5 p.m., sharp, and don't be late."

The meeting starts promptly at 5 p.m. Absent handshakes or verbal greetings, Ms. Parchisi (actress) starts by telling the two men, "You took my client's money, but have failed to get his bail reduced in order for him to manage his business and enjoy the fruits of his labor, gentlemen. He's angry and believes that your failure might be intentional. Your Binding Contract Agreement spells out the consequences of your failure."

"It's then that both men have an epiphany: They don't have in their possession the signed Binding Contract Agreement. The contracts were left behind in the excitement and haste to depart a couple of nights ago with bundles of money.

James Mason quickly responds. "Although we had the right judge hold the bail reduction hearing, it's true that our effort failed."

Ms. Parchisi/the actress interrupts him, "Well, you do also know and understand the consequences of your failure, which is beyond my personal control?"

"Speaking for both of us, we clearly understand the consequences, but I request an opportunity to show good faith."

"What is that?" she asks.

"Until the trial begins, I'll arrange special conditions at the prison for your client."

"In what form would that take, sir?"

"Well, he'll be placed in a segregated population to avoid bullies, sexual predators, and just plain deviants. He'll also be assigned to a large private cell. I'll also arrange for much better food and reading material, along with private radio and television."

"Mr. Mason and Mr. Roberts, that's all very interesting, but I'll take this under advisement with my client."

"Before advising your client, please also tell him that as prosecutor for the case, I have broad and ranging powers."

"What exactly does that mean, Mr. Mason?" she asks.

"It means that I will personally pave the way to ensure your client's release by working with you and the court."

"Sir, I'll take it under advisement with my client, but please know and understand that my client is very impatient and is known to be impetuous. Good day, sir."

CHAPTER SIXTEEN

Early the next morning, the real Katherine visits her lover in the Orleans Parish Prison. As Kenneth enters the visiting room, she is glad to see he is clean-shaven and full of energy. He is expecting to hear good news regarding his bail and release from the prison. She shakes her head side to side while projecting a broad smile as Kenneth enters the small visiting room. She says, "Based on your charges, and just as I had anticipated, your bail will continue at the current level. We got everything else we wanted, though, which includes better food, private radio, and a TV, along with a large private cell."

He smiles broadly at her beautiful face. She is thirty-five years of age but has skin and complexion that gave her a much younger and sophisticated appearance. "Sweetie, that's great. I appreciate your love, commitment, kindness, and all you've done for me. I have a plan leaning forward."

"What might that be, sweetie?"

"There are two things on my mind at this point in time, the first of which is in the form of another request of you. Would you arrange for us to be married here in prison?"

"What, oh goodness!" Katherine gasps in surprise, and without hesitation, gives her answer, "Of course I will! I want to be your wife."

This effort is aimed at hopefully rendering her immune and shielding her from testifying in a court of law about anything they've discussed related to his crimes and incarceration.

The next morning, Katherine contacts the Protestant minister, Richard Brock, who is assigned to the prison to provide inmates with spiritual guidance and support.

"Chaplain Brock, good morning, my name is Katherine Parchisi. I've contacted you because my fiancé and I would like you to perform our marriage ceremony. He's currently a prisoner at Orleans Parish Prison."

"What is the inmate's name?"

"Kenneth Blanchard."

"Thank you, I'll have to counsel with the inmate before proceeding further. The prison warden must also sanction the request for marriage on the grounds of the prison. Are you certain that he is receptive to your holy wedlock?"

"Yes, Chaplain I'm absolutely certain that he is quite receptive. I'm sure you'll confirm that with him before conducting the ceremony. Would you be kind enough to accommodate us?"

"Yes, I would, assuming a marriage license can be obtained and approval is secured from the warden."

"Chaplin Brock, earlier this morning, I secured a marriage license from the Parish Clerk's Office."

Because of the unusual request, Chaplain Brock refers to prison policy, which does not discriminate against legal marriage conducted within the walls of the prison.

From within the visiting room, the ceremony is about to start. Noticeably missing are the usual wedding decorations, flowers, and formally clad bridal party. The only guests present for the ceremony are Kenneth's friend from college, Randy Wade, who is now the chief of security. Chaplain Brock conducts the marriage ceremony while Kenneth and Katherine stand at opposite ends of the table, where they would normally be seated. There is no exchange of wedding rings or allowance for the customary embrace.

The sparse ceremony is over less than five minutes after Chaplain Brock pronounces them husband and wife. Although human contact between the newlyweds is prohibited, Kenneth is pleased because his bride is now legally shielded from being compelled to testify in a court of law about interactions between the two of them. However, being married to Katherine is bittersweet. Blanchard knows that they will never experience wedded bliss.

Shortly after the wedding, on a chilly evening in March, Kenneth Blanchard sits down at a small makeshift writing surface in his private prison cell and starts to write:

"My name is Kenneth Blanchard. As my final act, let it be known that I have committed several brutal slayings of 3 human beings. The victims are Jason Beale, Julius Raymond, and Detective David Stoddard. I have also confessed to this as detailed in a Binding Contract Agreement between District Attorney James Mason, Chief of Police George Roberts, and myself. My longtime attorney, who is currently representing me for deaths of those 3 human beings, will upon my death, submit the fully executed Binding Contract Agreement to the appropriate law enforcement official of jurisdiction for review and action disposition.

"The terms and conditions of the Binding Contract Agreement clearly outline an illegal enterprise and conspiracy on the part of District Attorney James Mason and Chief of Police George Roberts, who conspired with me to manipulate the courts and the whole of the legal justice system, purely for purposes of avarice and personal gain. These two criminals, as I've described them herein, were so preoccupied with bundling up $1,000,000 in cash, that they failed to take with them a copy of the fully executed Binding Contract Agreement. Their complicity in perpetrating crime(s) of criminal conspiracy is patently clear. I'm certain that the U.S. Attorney and the Internal Revenue Service will want to speak with District Attorney James Mason and Chief of Police George Roberts, if they don't commit suicide before such an event might occur.

"Please also know and understand that these 2 conspirators, District Attorney James Mason and Chief of Police George Roberts, who plotted to manipulate the U.S. justice system, have been captured on videotape and voice monitoring as they discussed a scheme to receive money in exchange for arranging reduction in bail for me, and that if I were ever convicted, I would be sentenced to no more than 5 years served in a minimum-security facility. These documented events occurred at my residence, located at 5944 Argonne Boulevard, New Orleans. As a bribe, District Attorney James Mason and Chief of Police George Roberts accepted equal amounts of ill-gotten gains, totaling

$1,000,000, as an inducement to manipulate the U.S. Criminal Justice System.

"By the time this confession is read by an appropriate law enforcement official, my spirit will have passed on to another dimension, in death. Do the right thing

Headliner News Flash

Kenneth Blanchard, a prominent entrepreneur who was being held in the Orleans Parish Prison as a suspect on a triple homicide warrant, was discovered dead in his prison cell today. According to the medical examiner's preliminary report, Mr. Blanchard died as a result of hanging by the neck from within his prison cell. Reportedly, Mr. Blanchard was the sole occupant of the prison cell. According to prison officials, Mr. Blanchard's death is currently under investigation. Although unconfirmed, there is reason to suspect that a suicide note was found in his cell, the contents of which are unknown. Mr. Blanchard is survived by his wife, Katherine. The body was released to Frazier's Mortuary. The date of the funeral has not been determined.

EPILOGUE

Kenneth Blanchard is now on another dimension, Katherine has mourned his loss, but she is now ready to begin living her life to the fullest. She leaves FA&O, opting to travel the world over land, sea, and air conveyance to experience, and enjoy the world. She splurges on anything that suits her fancy and makes her happy. She has the ability to do this because of her unbridled access to millions of dollars in cold hard cash, compliments of Kenneth Blanchard's "stash." Eventually, she settles in the South of France. There, she has purchased a fabulous mansion estate, where the climate and environment is ideal. She dines regularly at hilltop towns where Micheline-starred restaurants are featured. Given her natural beauty, men can't help but noticed and take long looks at her exquisite physique and gorgeous bronzed complexion. She finds love in a wealthy astrophysicist from Africa, who courts her on a regular basis. Katherine generously gives to worthy causes, especially those benefitting women and children. She dabbles minimally in real estate and other opportunities for wise investment.

She never forgot the invaluable role the actress, Consuela, played in implicating George Roberts and James Mason for their conspiracy, greed, blind political ambition, and manipulation of the Criminal Justice System. They both are now in the custody of the Federal Bureau of Prisons.

Sometime later, Greg Pardee called Art on the telephone, and asked about the availability of reward money, but was disappointed when Art informed him that the case had been solved. Art smiled broadly as he gave Greg the bad news. Greg grumbled loudly and slammed down the phone. Greg was forced to find a job to take care of himself, rather than relying upon the generosity of others.

Dimi and Nadia Ivanov were headed out to sea to settle at their retirement Shangri-La, when they were stopped and arrested by agents of the Federal Bureau of Investigation. They are currently serving lengthy prison sentences for a variety of crimes.

Although Consuela was promised a bonus payment of ten-thousand dollars, Katherine opted to award her with one-hundred thousand dollars, in cash.

Eventually, Art was selected as Chief of Police, and Jeff is now Chief of the Homicide Division.

-ABOUT THE AUTHOR-

Robert is a graduate of the University of San Francisco, where he earned a Bachelor of Science Degree majoring in Human Relations and Organizational Behavior. He went on to focus on a master's degree, with a concentration in Public Administration. He used his skills to help guide the careers of junior and mid-level managers.

Robert comes from a large family, many of whom live in the vicinity of Washington, D.C., where he grew up. He served in the U.S. Army for 20 years until retirement in 1985. Robert went on to serve for 30 years in a variety of positions as a civilian Federal employee. He and his wife, Maria, make their home in the San Francisco Bay Area.

As a 32nd degree Freemason, Robert is a member of Torri Lodge #46. He is also a member of Obelisk Temple of Keystone Consistory #225, based at Okinawa, Japan.

www.ingramcontent.com/pod-product-compliance
Lightning Source LLC
Chambersburg PA
CBHW071252130626
46556CB00003B/1277